Paladin

JENNIFER ELAINE

Dedicated to the real Sean and Vivi.

*Thank you for being my sanity and insanity
all
at the same time.*

*All the art of living lies in a fine mingling
of letting go and holding on.*
-Havelock Ellis

TABLE OF CONTENTS

Chapter 1

*R*un! That was all Sean heard. *Run!* The voice got louder in his head. *Run!* He couldn't see his family anymore, only the front door. *Run!* So, he did.

He ran past everyone. He threw the door wide open and raced down the front steps of the house. He rushed past the Banners, who lived three houses from his own. Mr. Banner was watering his lawn when a blur went past him. Sean sped across streets, not worrying about cars. Not worrying about getting hurt. Not worrying about anything. There wasn't another thought inside his head besides *run.*

After ten minutes his legs began to throb, but it only pushed him to go faster. He ran past the park where he would play baseball with his friends, past the store where his mother would go for the little things that she would forget at the major supermarket, and past the gas station where his... The thought came to him. Sean pictured himself sitting in the car, while his... He couldn't bear the thought of the man pumping gas. Tears began running down his face. He couldn't stop them. He couldn't take it. He didn't want it to be true. He didn't want it to be real. He was not in control. He was not Sean anymore. He turned his head and saw a bus coming through the corner of his eye. *The driver won't have enough time to react*, he thought. *Then it will be over. The pain will be gone*. He started charging toward the street. *Just a few more feet. Just a few more seconds. Just a few more inches now.*

In a flash, she grabbed him. She came out of nowhere. Held him as tightly as she could. His mother was stronger than she looked. Five-foot-three and only half a foot taller than Sean. She just held him. Not saying a word. Sean gave in and stopped fighting her. He let his body relax in her arms. He didn't know how much time had gone by, but she suddenly pulled away. Tears filled her already exhausted eyes. She shook her head and said, "I know but...you can't. Okay? You just can't." She held him again. She took his hand and led him slowly back to the house. Sean didn't think of it as home. Not anymore. How could it be home without him? They said nothing else to each other for the rest of the walk. It felt like hours to Sean.

When their house was finally in sight, Sean could see his Uncle Leo standing outside, keeping watch over his sister at the top of the stairs. He couldn't remember if Leo had been in the room when she had told him. It was all a fog. He had to have been there, though, because Leo was the one who picked him up from school. Sean remembered that; he remembered the solemn behavior of his uncle. He remembered thinking it was strange because Leo was known as the goofball in the family. The dork, the clown, the one always laughing and making jokes. Even his appearance invited you to laugh. He was a giant, for starters. A giant to Sean anyway. He wasn't sure how tall his uncle was, just that he was the tallest in the family. Way taller than his mom and even taller than... *No,* he thought. *I can't think about him.* As tall as Leo was, he only looked taller because of his lanky stature. He had light brown hair that was beginning to recede into an M shape on his head. But the thing that really stood out to Sean about Leo was that permanent smirk that always covered his face. A smirk that Sean realized today was not permanent.

As they started walking up the first set of stairs, Sean heard that familiar little voice. "Shen, where you go?" She let go of Leo's hand and met them halfway. She reached out for him with her little hands. Sean couldn't even look at her. How could he? Viviana had his eyes. Big round light eyes. The kind of eyes that change color from green to blue and back again according to their mood. She threw her arms around his leg. Everyone was acting differently. His mom, his uncle, himself, but not Viviana. She was the same. Of course she was the same, she was only two. Not old enough to understand what happened. Not old enough to understand what was lost. With the help of his mother and uncle, Sean pulled her off as gently as possible, and then went straight to his room. He laid there in silence waiting for the day to be over. He pulled the blankets over his head, hiding from his family, from the world, but most importantly hiding from the truth.

That night the bad dreams started.

Chapter 2

The next morning, Sean only came out of his room to use the bathroom. He didn't watch any TV, play any video games, or respond to anyone in the house, which seemed to be his entire family. Aunts, uncles, grandparents, and cousins were all there. Even Nana B was there. She must have driven all through the night. Usually, Sean would be excited about seeing her and her boyfriend, Larry. But not this time. Maybe never again the way Sean felt. They and everyone else tried to talk to him, but his Uncle Leo acted like a bodyguard. Every time someone knocked on his door with a "Hey Buddy," "Sweetheart," or "Sean, Honey," the next thing heard was Leo's voice telling them he was resting.

His mother had left a sandwich on his nightstand from lunch. The smell of ham and cheese lingered in his room. Sean dragged himself out of bed and walked over to the only mirror in his room, which rested on top of his dresser. The dresser was high, so Sean could only see to his top lip and above. He looked into his light brown eyes, staring from one to the other. They were like his mother's but bigger. His tan skin looked paler, but his cheeks were still chubby. Something he was self-conscious about. Though everyone would say it was just baby fat, he was still teased about it at school. He swallowed hard and felt a pain in the back of his throat.

Sean realized from the length of his shadow coming from the window light that it must be late in the afternoon. He walked over to the window. He saw the sun's rays peeking from the clouds. He saw his neighbor, Mr. Wayne, washing his car. Sean could hear children playing outside, although he could not see them.

It all seemed so strange to Sean. How was Mr. Wayne washing his car? How were the kids playing? How did the sun come up? All of it should have stopped. How could his life go on without him? How could anyone's life go on, go on like nothing had happened? "He was killed yesterday," he whispered. "He was killed," he repeated still in a whisper. He banged on the glass. Louder this time, "My father was killed yesterday." Hitting the glass, again and again, echoing the same words.

Mr. Wayne, at the sound and sight of Sean in the window, turned off his hose. Screaming now, "My father was killed yesterday!" The children couldn't be heard playing anymore. "My father was killed!" His mother threw open the door and rushed to him. She pulled him away from the window. Sean's eyes were watering from the pain, but he was still screaming. No words this time. Just screams.

"Sean, please," his mother pleaded to get him to calm down. Probably weakened from her state of mind, she was no match for the struggle Sean was putting up. He managed to pry himself from her grip. Before anyone in the house could react, Sean was out the door, running down the stairs, barefoot in his school clothes from the day before.

And so, it went every day, the same result. Seeing mail with his father's name, Robert O'Leary, his friends coming by to give their condolences or to check in on Sean, his sister asking, "Where papa? Where papa?" It all sent Sean spiraling out of control and out the door. It didn't matter what he was wearing or who saw him. It didn't matter if it was early or late. None of it mattered anymore, except running. He needed to get out. He needed to get away. He needed to run.

Chapter 3

*T*he principal, teachers, and his baseball coach all understood and did not question his absence in any way. Running was the only time Sean left the house for the last week. His mother did not push except for one particular day. She had spoken to him about not going out for this one particular day. That day had now come. It was surreal to him and everyone else, aside from Viviana, who was left to her innocent bubble. Viviana, or Vivi as the family fondly referred to her, was quietly sitting watching Scooby-doo while holding her favorite stuffed animal, Figaro. Sean could hear the cartoon in the background as he stared at himself in his mom's full-length mirror. His suit was navy blue with a black tie. He had worn it once before but did not remember when. It fit him better now, though. His mother offered to buy him something new, but she couldn't get a straight answer from him. He was wearing new dress shoes. Or at least new for him. They were hand-me-downs from the neighbor's son across the street. They were too big. Sean never let that fact be known to anyone though. He hadn't let much be known lately.

His mother walked in with a long black dress that went past her knees. It didn't look new, but Sean didn't remember seeing it before. *Maybe it's a hand-me-down also*, he thought. His mother was getting so many items from everyone, family, of course, the neighbors, mom's friends, the base. They had made so much food for Sean's family that their freezer was packed, and his mother wouldn't need to cook for the next week or so. His mother gave him a forced half-smile and asked how the suit fit. Sean nodded and his mother had to accept that as an answer.

The phone began ringing. Sean knew it was his uncle before his mother answered. "No, we'll meet you at the church. I'm not done getting Vivi ready," she paused. "Okay, yes." His mother began walking down the hallway into Vivi's room. Sean could hear her voice becoming more distant. "See you there, love you too."

"Loretta, are the kids almost ready?" asked Nana B from the guest room.

"I need to fix Vivi's hair," she pulled a hair tie off her wrist. "Mom, there were no black dresses in her size at the mall so the darkest dress we have for her is the purple dress that has a green caterpillar on it."

Sean leaned against the doorway facing out of the room.

"That's fine. People will understand and if they don't, well then the hell with them."

Loretta breathed out hard and responded with, "Okay, mom."

Nana B was straightening Larry's tie for him. "And for Sean?"

"He's wearing the same suit from the Christmas pictures."

Sean moved his eyes off the floor to the Christmas picture in the hallway, hanging next to a black-and-white painting of his mother's favorite flower, the orchid. There was Sean in his suit holding Viviana on his lap, while his mother and father embraced each other behind them. Sean was gone before anyone realized.

Luckily, Nana B finished getting Vivi ready, while Loretta went looking for her son. They were a few minutes late to the proceedings, but who would dare comment on such a trivial thing on such a monumental day? No one at that church. There were so many people inside that there weren't enough pews for everyone, and many had to stand in the back. Most of them were soldiers, dressed in their blues. But Sean didn't notice. He let himself be preoccupied only with the pain he experienced from the dress shoes. He felt a blister pop on his right foot. He focused on that, not wanting to pay attention to anything else. The idea was working just fine. If you asked him which priest was performing the funeral, he wouldn't even be able to tell you, and he knew all the priests. Sunday service had been a tradition in their family for as long as he could remember. He had plans to become an altar boy in two years when he turned twelve. He squeezed his toes on his left foot and focused on a new blister that was forming.

Sean was distracted until his sister got down from the pew and went running up to the altar. Loretta was too lost in her own thoughts to notice Vivi was up initially. Sean's eyes went wide open as he watched his sister go straight to their father's eleven by fourteen Naval portrait. She put her little hand on the picture and let out a small sigh that made everyone in the church gasp in sympathy. The sound brought Loretta back to reality. She rushed up to comfort her little one, as she watched the church doors close. She already knew without looking who it was that had left. She glanced over at her brother. Leo stood up staring, waiting for some direction on what he should do to help, but Loretta just took a deep breath and walked slowly back to her seat while holding Vivi in her arms.

Chapter 4

Sean stared at the painting on the wall. It was a picture of a path that seemed to wind up a mountain. Sean thought about how it might feel to run up that mountain. He imagined the cold dry air filling his lungs. It had been weeks now of the running. Before he would run when playing games with his friends, during baseball practice, or for gym class. Now running was something else. Something that could not be described. Something Sean felt he needed. Something that made Loretta make this appointment. He stared for another minute while his mother spoke in the background.

"It was the school who recommended you. He... Sean is getting into trouble for running out of class and the school..."

Sean's eyes followed down to the desk underneath the painting. The desk was neat, holding up only a few items. A cordless phone, pens in a pencil holder, a picture inside a frame of two boys finger painting, a notepad, and a nameplate that read "Dr. Prince."

"Please go on," said Dr. Prince.

"That's pretty much the main issue. So..." Loretta was fidgeting with her wedding ring. "Do I stay here or... "

After a short moment of reflection, Dr. Prince said, "I think it would be best if I talk to Sean alone now."

"Okay." Loretta looked at Sean for a moment, at the doctor, and then back at Sean, before kissing the side of his head. She whispered in his ear, "Just try to..." Her voice broke a little. "Just try."

Sean nodded to appease her. He began staring at the painting again, studying the details.

"We'll be fine, Mrs. O'Leary." Dr. Prince smiled genuinely.

Loretta grabbed her purse and walked quietly to the door. She closed it behind her, then closed her eyes before she said a silent prayer to herself. After pulling her car keys out of her purse, she exited the hallway.

There was silence for some time. Dr. Prince was waiting for Sean to make eye contact, but Sean wasn't there. He was on the mountain, running in the open air, not inside a closed office.

"Do you like the painting?"

Sean was brought back by the break of silence.

Dr. Prince repeated the question.

Sean nodded.

"I love the mountains. I grew up in Colorado." She paused for a moment. "Have you ever been there? Colorado?"

"Yes," Sean said without overthinking it.

"And to the mountains?"

Sean finally lowered his eyes to look at her. She was an older woman. He couldn't tell her age, just that she was older than his mother. She wore silver glasses that made her soft brown eyes larger. *She looks like she would give good candy during Halloween,* Sean thought. The kind of candy that his friends and he would hunt the neighborhood for.

Sean missed his friends, but it wasn't the same with them. The two times that Sean went and hung out with them, he felt like an alien in a new world. Tommy, John, Vinny, and James tried to act normal around Sean, but they were afraid to say the wrong thing. The whole time it was like they were walking on eggshells around him. It didn't make him feel better. Honestly, if they had acted like nothing had changed it wouldn't have made him feel better either, because, well, things had changed. Everything was different now.

"Sean? Did you hear my question? Have you ever been to the mountains?"

Sean found himself feeling envious of them. Well, all of them except for Vinny, who hadn't seen his dad in years. But Sean thought at that moment, *I'd rather have that.* He would rather have a dad who was alive and was some deadbeat, instead of this. Maybe if his dad wasn't so good, maybe if they hadn't been so close, then maybe this wouldn't be so... *Run!*

Sean was out the door.

Chapter 5

Sean was back in Dr. Prince's office the next day. She had been extremely understanding about the rescheduling of their appointment.

This time Dr. Prince spoke immediately after Loretta left.

"So yesterday, we started talking about the painting, and well… That's as far as we got." She laughed lightly.

Sean was silent, staring at his shoes. He had to tie his left shoelace but felt frozen by the feel of the doctor's eyes on him. Dr. Prince tried again to get Sean to talk. "Was there something about the painting you didn't like?"

Sean shook his head. Dr. Prince asked if he wanted to discuss the painting more. Sean just shrugged his shoulders.

"You know, Sean, I'm here for you. We can talk about anything you like. Anything at all, baseball, video games, movies, books... running."

Sean's eyes met hers when he heard the last word. That was why his mother brought him there. Sean knew that his mother merely tolerated the running. He knew deep down she wanted it to stop. He overheard her talking to her friends, Liz and Melissa, about how she wished his school had a track team or something, anything to focus the running. Sean didn't run for fun or sport though.

"Tell me why you run, Sean."

"I..." Sean hadn't thought about it much, he would feel overwhelmed then his legs would start moving. "I...," he breathed out. He did not know how to fully explain why he ran.

Dr. Prince nodded. "I think I understand Sean. I actually run myself. I do. I find it relaxing. How much do you run?"

"I don't know," Sean answered easily.

"I run at least twice a week." Dr. Prince was careful to keep the conversation light. Her goal was to get him to stay the entire session.

And so, went the visits between Sean and the doctor. He saw her three times a week after school. Some sessions Sean stayed the whole time, and others, Dr. Prince brought up his father. The running didn't seem to be slowing down.

Chapter 6

Sean could hear his mom talking to Leo while packing Vivi's room up.

"You have to understand. This is what we all need." Sean moved closer to the room. He could see them both, but they were too pre-occupied to notice him. His mother looked so small next to Leo. Truly, you wouldn't even know the two were related. They didn't look a thing alike. They did both have light brown hair and light brown eyes, but Loretta had softer features, and most notably a softer smile. She had a way of making everyone feel comfortable with that smile, no matter who they were. Many had made the mistake of connecting her looks with her personality. Yes, she was kind and laid back, but thinking she was a pushover would be a grand misjudgment of her strength. After all, she had an older brother who'd shown her the ropes. That is what

Sean always heard anyway. His mother had to hold her own growing up because she was the only girl in a sea of boys since all her cousins were males. Leo always took her everywhere with him. Loretta joked at times that it was her brother who raised her, which made Leo grin ear-to-ear, but she wouldn't dare make that joke in front of Nana B.

Leo wasn't smiling now. Sean had seen a lot of people not smiling lately.

"Look, I can't do it anymore," Loretta blurted out.

"Do what?"

"Do what? Are you kidding me?" She stopped and stared at him. She waved her arms around. "This. I can't do this. Any of it. I can't go to the supermarket, the gas station, the mall." She looked away and began folding one of Vivi's shirts that had lace trim around it. "The bank," she said, her voice cracking.

The death was never fully explained to Sean. He knew he was not ready to hear it, but it was unclear to him whether his mother was even ready to say it. All he knew was that his father had only been back from tour for a day and was running errands, an oil change for the jeep, pick up some dry cleaning, and the bank. The bank was to be the last stop before he would pick Sean up early from school.

Sean remembered that day. He had been overwhelmed with excitement when they paged his name on the loudspeaker at school. "Mrs. Frost, Sean O'Leary for early dismissal." Sean beamed as he began packing up. Not only was he getting picked up early, but he was also sure it would be his dad getting him for a day of fun. His father had come in late the night before. Sean and Vivi were already asleep. That morning on the drive to school was when his mother announced that their father was home. He'd perked up in the car from the news that his dad would be the one picking him up around lunchtime. During school, he had obsessively checked his watch to see how many more hours until his father would come for him.

When he left the classroom, he had strutted all the way down the hall, even waved to other classes on the way. That is until he saw the solemn looks of everyone in the office. No one said a word about what happened. A look of disappointment washed over Sean's face when he saw his uncle. Leo didn't say much to him except that it was important to go, and they really needed to get home. Sean wondered why he seemed so upset. Sean let his mind wander in the silence of the car ride home. Maybe the

Yankees lost a game. He couldn't remember if they had a game last night. Maybe Aunt Toni was mad about him not helping around the house. That wouldn't be the first time. Or maybe his father and uncle got into some kind of dispute. No, they always got along. If anything, the two would team up against everyone else in the family. He didn't think for a moment that it could be what it turned out to be. Why would it be? His dad was home from a tour. It was only dangerous when he was away.

The memory washed over Sean like a tsunami. He felt like he couldn't breathe. And there it was, the voice, *Run!* Like the wind, he was gone.

Loretta heard the door slam and leaned toward the window to see Sean sprinting down the street in his pajamas. Throwing the shirt down on the bed and biting her lip to keep from crying, she said, "And there's that."

Leo got up from the bed to see the last glimpse of Sean before he was out of sight.

"The therapy isn't helping?" he asked, still staring out the window.

"It's been over a year of seeing her and he's still running. Dr. Prince says it's normal, but...," holding back tears she continued, "I lost Robert. I can't lose Sean, too. And I feel like if we stay here, we're stuck in the same cycle." She paused. "I want my son…" Tears were falling down her cheeks as she forced the words out. "I want my son back, okay."

Leo went to Loretta and held her tightly.

"But Virginia is so far away," he whispered.

"It's not that far."

He pulled away from her, but still held on to his baby sister. "How am I supposed to help you from there? How can I be there for you and the kids? Right now you are just a bridge away."

"Leo, I love you, but I'm your sister, not your responsibility. You have your own wife and kids to worry about." She sat on Vivi's bed, picked up the same shirt again, and held it in her hands.

Leo sat down next to her. "Is that what this is about? You think Toni cares about me helping you? She knows how hard this has been for you."

Loretta put her hands over her face, then pulled them down and took a deep breath. "It has been hard," she nodded. "And it's been almost two years and it hasn't gotten any easier. Sean is still running out there whenever he feels any emotion or... anything at all, and Vivi. I want Vivi to have some sense of normalcy."

"You always said being normal was boring." His smirk was back on his face. "Besides, moving hundreds of miles away is not going to stop me from worrying about you. Especially now that you're moving back in with mom."

Loretta let out a small laugh of relief and grabbed his hand.

"I just want to make sure you're okay," he said in a somber voice.

"I'm not okay." She swallowed hard. "Staying here I won't be. Not right now anyway. I am suffocating here. He's... everywhere. I can't have him, and I can't get away from him," she paused. "Does that make me sound horrible?"

"No, it doesn't," Leo responded without hesitation.

"Look, I don't know if going up there will make a difference, but I need a change." Her eyes hit the floor.

He wrapped his arm around her shoulder. "Okay."

She looked up at him.

"I'm not happy about this. But okay. I get it," he paused. "For now."

Chapter 7

Sean was waiting in the jeep. His sister was getting hugs and kisses from their cousins. Sean could see out of his peripheral vision that his uncle was coming to the car door. He rolled down the window for Leo.

"Hey, so your aunt is making me clean out a lot of my 'junk,' as she puts it. And I found these old comics and I figured, since I was blessed with three girls, that maybe you'd wanna keep them."

Sean tried his best to smile for him.

"It's my favorite superhero. Paladin."

Sean took the stack of comics from him and looked them over.

"There's twelve of them there," he said. "You know the legend is that he was a real guy a hundred or something years ago."

A comment like that would usually make Sean bring his eyebrows down in skepticism, but instead, he just nodded trying to get to the end of the conversation.

"No one knows what happened to him." Leo gave his famous smirk.

Sean couldn't distinguish whether Leo truly believed what he said or if it was just another failed attempt to be playful with him like he used to be. Sean was indifferent either way.

"Thanks." Sean forced a smile again and briefly made eye contact.

"You know you can call me whenever. I don't care the time. In the middle of the night, early morning, when the Yankees are playing." Leo gave a big smile. "Whenever. Okay?"

Sean nodded while tucking in his lips but didn't look at him.

"Okay. I'm not going to make you get out of the car so... " He put his hand out.

They shook. "Alright," he said. "Take care of your mom and sister."

"Okay."

"Love you."

"I know."

"Okay, Han."

Sean got the reference, but all he wanted was to stop talking, so he picked up one of the comics and pretended to read. Leo tried not to look hurt as he walked over to give Loretta and Vivi their goodbyes. It all became background noise to Sean. Loretta strapped Vivi into her car seat.

"You guys ready to go," she said as she climbed into the driver's seat.

"Weady," Vivi called out excitedly.

Loretta started the ignition and waved goodbye. As she pulled out onto the road, Sean waited until they were out of sight to throw the comic books in a box behind him. He put his Walkman on and watched as everything familiar to him slowly disappeared.

Chapter 8

Sean didn't know how many hours it was to Nana B's house. His mother did tell him, but he wasn't listening at that moment. They stopped periodically for food, bathroom breaks, and stretching. After more than six hours on and off the road, Sean was more than bored. The batteries in his Walkman had died a long time ago and his mom was playing Disney movie songs for Vivi. He was in and out of consciousness for a while, but now he yearned just to be out of the car. His muscles were aching to run. His body had adapted to it. He had grown more than two inches in the last eight months. Sean could now see his entire face in the mirror on top of his dresser. And as for the baby fat that he was sporadically teased about, well, that was long gone. His mom always looked sad when people said he no longer looked like a baby. Another change she was not ready for.

He turned around aggressively to find… something, anything. He picked up the comics that Leo gave him. He wasn't really interested, but he was desperate at that point. He had to block out the sound of Ariel singing "Part of Your World." He perused them to find one that looked the least lame. He found one titled *Paladin, the Outlaw Issue 12*. On the cover was an image of a man with his back to an angry mob. Sean decided that reading them in order didn't matter. He just wanted to pass the time and the idea of a superhero turning bad seemed different to him.

Sean breezed through the comic. Then he slowly became engulfed by the idea that a man who was so beloved could become hated without a thought about loyalty, compassion, or respect. The same people whom Paladin protected and saved turned on him the moment propaganda showed him in a bad light. They were fueled by people's prejudices and fear. And in the end, Paladin saved the day again despite it all. Sean went back for another comic book. This time he went for the first issue simply titled *Paladin*. He wanted to know where Paladin came from, why he was here, and how he got his powers. He wanted to know his origin story. *Was he an alien like Superman, a soldier like Captain America, or a scientist like Hulk?* There was an image of a boy around Sean's age with the shadow of a man on the cover. Sean was slightly disappointed to learn that the first edition did not give any of these details besides his age when he became a hero.

Sean did discover that even as a child Paladin had a fighting spirit. Sean guessed from their clothes and speech that the setting was long ago. Paladin had a bo staff with him that he always used named Verendus. *Much easier to remember than Thor's hammer*, Sean thought. There was an epic battle between Paladin and some villain named Nefarian. Paladin was the underdog, but he slayed his Goliath. The story absorbed Sean. He continued with the other issues.

Chapter 9

They were thirty minutes from Virginia, and by now Sean had read each comic book at least twice. It didn't matter if they were driving, stopped at a gas station, or a diner. Sean was reading. Loretta didn't say a word, she was just happy she didn't have to worry about him running off and getting lost. Sean was mesmerized by each word, each graphic, each victory. Paladin battled Hirendan three times. That was his archnemesis. He was a human who was obsessed with killing Paladin so that he could be the world's savior. Sean watched Paladin grow through the issues. No longer a boy when he finally defeated Hirendan for the last time. Peace did not last long though for Hirendan's son Iniquan took on the torch. Each comic seemed to take place in a different decade or longer. *That would make him over a hundred and twenty years old. Is he immor-*

tal? Or does he just age slowly? Sean wondered these questions and more.

Sean had never liked comic books before. Sure, he watched and enjoyed the Batman and Superman shows. He even watched the Fantastic Four reruns with his friends, but when it came to the comics, he was always more interested in playing video games or baseball. Paladin was different, there was something about him that drew Sean in. He seemed so real. He matured, grew, and evolved. Slowly through the editions, Paladin was ready to give it all up. He didn't want to be a hero anymore; he was being forced into it. He desperately wanted to be normal. Paladin struggled again and again with his unwanted powers. Sean could understand wanting to give it up after the twelfth issue when the people had turned on him, but Paladin wanted to leave it all behind long before that. Sean found him to be selfish. He found him to be narrow-minded. He found him to be like everybody else. Sean thought *Paladin is already what he wants.* He was just as human as anyone on the planet, just with powers.

Sean stared outside at the night sky and wondered why the creator would design such a flawed character.

"We're here," his mother said. Her voice sounded tired.

Sean felt like he was waking from a dream. He could suddenly hear the lyrics to "A Dream is a Wish Your Heart Makes." He turned to see that his sister had passed out holding Figaro. Then he turned the other way to see Nana B and Larry coming out to greet them.

"The prodigal daughter returns," Larry joked as he hugged Loretta. Sean opened the door to be attacked by hugs and kisses. Nana B went on and on about how big he'd gotten. Sean stretched as he looked around his surroundings. It had been a while since he visited Virginia, but the house was exactly how he remembered it. Brown, two stories with a large porch, and a wide yard set directly on the corner of Marvel Avenue. Even the house across the street looked the same, except it had a "For Sale" sign on it now that he could barely read because of the flickering streetlight above his head. Sean swore he recalled the same light struggling the last time he was there. On the north side across the street and on the south side next to their property were matching long patches of trees giving Larry and Nana B plenty of privacy.

"Sean, just grab what you need for tonight, we can get the rest tomorrow," Loretta said as she picked Vivi up.

Sean grabbed a small suitcase where he knew his toothbrush was and gently placed his newly prized possessions inside. *I may need to read them again*, he thought. Larry helped by grabbing some bags while Nana B held the door open for them all.

Chapter 10

The next day Sean woke up early. He hadn't slept well in some time. Last night his mind just wouldn't turn off, but to him, it was better that way. Better than having the nightmares. His mind was spinning with the images, graphics, and tales of Paladin. He picked up the phone and called Leo.

"Hey buddy, how was the trip?"

"It was fine," Sean responded quickly.

"Everything okay?"

"Yes… I wanted to ask you about the Paladin comics."

"Liked them, huh? Yeah, I was obsessed with them when I was your age."

Sean waited patiently for his turn to talk.

"I even had a poster hanging in my room."

"Uncle Leo?"

"Yeah, Sean?"

"Do you have any other issues? Maybe somewhere in your garage?"

"Oh no, definitely not. There were only thirteen. I never got my hands on the last one either. To be honest, Paladin was not the most popular comic book back then, so most places didn't even carry them. I was lucky to get the twelve I had." There was silence for a moment. "I'm sorry, Sean."

"It's okay. Do you know the name of the last edition?"

"Um...," he paused for a second. "I think, if I remember correctly, it was called *The Death of Peace*."

The words sunk into Sean's head as they made connections to memories. The memories drowned out everything else Leo said. He tried to ignore it and focus on Leo's voice, but the voice inside his head was louder.

"Are you still there, Sean? Can you hear me? Sean?"

The phone was left off the hook while Sean's legs explored new territory.

Chapter 11

Loretta was up by the time Sean got back.

"Sit," was the word he was greeted with.

Sean knew it was best just to do what she said when she used commands like that.

"Sean, we are going to have to come up with some ground rules for your running."

He looked at her, which was enough of a response for her to continue.

"There are back streets to this neighborhood with bicycle lanes that you may have noticed."

Sean kept his eye contact.

"You are to use those streets and be in those bicycle lanes when you go for your runs."

He looked away.

"This is not up for negotiation or debate," she affirmed.

Sean looked at her and nodded.

"No. I'm going to need to hear a verbal confirmation of these rules." Her voice was firm.

"I understand," he mumbled and then looked away.

"The phone was off the hook when I got up. When I hung it back up, Leo called. He was worried after... apparently you guys got disconnected or something." Her tone showed that she didn't believe the words. "He wanted me to tell you that maybe trying some local comic book stores might be a good idea."

Sean drank some water while his mother continued.

"So, you enjoyed them?" She paused for a second but then continued realizing a response was unlikely. "That's really good, Sean. I'm glad." She walked over to him and leaned against the sink with her back. "Hey, wanna take a ride with me to the grocery store?"

Sean was about to say no when he heard his mother proceed with, "maybe we'll see some comic book stores on the way."

*****

Sean watched the green scenery go by as they drove. There were more trees there than in his old neighborhood. Sean scanned the area closely for anything that resembled a comic book store without luck.

"Come inside and pick out some things you want," Loretta said while parking the jeep.

Sean walked slowly around the aisles while his mother compared prices.

"Things are a lot cheaper out here than back home huh?"

Sean pretended not to hear her. Eventually, they made their way to the deli department. Loretta grabbed a ticket to get some cold cuts. From the corner of his eye, Sean saw a tall man with a baseball hat on. He recognized the Cavaliers logo. His hair, peeking out from the back, was brown, but his thick beard was a more reddish tone. The man turned his head in their direction, but due to the reflective glasses the man was wearing, Sean couldn't tell if he was looking at them or not. That is until a single nod was given. Typically, Sean would return the male greeting, but instead, he looked away abruptly, not wanting to make any kind of connection.

The man behind the deli counter called the next number.

"Is that you, Rick?"

The deepest voice Sean ever heard then spoke. "It is, but the lady can go first." He gestured towards Loretta. "You know I have no place to go anyway."

"Always the gentleman," the deli man remarked, tilting his head in Rick's direction.

"That's okay, you were here first," Loretta said.

"I insist." His accent wasn't like the deli man's, Nana B's, or Larry's.

He must not be from around here, Sean thought.

"Are you sure? I have a pretty long list."

Rick didn't respond except for a signal with his left hand for her to step forward.

"Ma'am, this guy doesn't take no for an answer," the deli man said, pointing to Rick. "Now what can I get for ya?"

While Loretta ordered Sean's, Vivi's, and Larry's favorite meats and cheeses, Sean studied Rick more closely. There was something different about him. He couldn't yet put his finger on it. Was it the huge belt buckle? Maybe it was his T-shirt that was two sizes too small around the arms? *Probably on purpose,* was Sean's thought. Or it could be the way he was tapping his index finger on the glass while browsing the deli choices? Whatever the reason, Sean felt it and he felt it strongly. And because he couldn't explain it, Sean filed it as hatred. It was the first emotion in a long time that didn't make Sean go running out the door.

When Loretta finished, she thanked Rick again. Rick smiled and nodded. Loretta began to move her cart to the closest aisle to obtain the next item on her list, while Sean stayed behind, still somewhat confused by this emotion.

"Always a sucker for a looker?"

Sean's eyes narrowed as he realized they were talking about his mother.

"Just trying to show that chivalry isn't dead yet, Frank." Rick paused for a moment then said, "I haven't seen her around here before. She must be new."

Frank whispered while smiling, "Well, ya know whose daughter that is?" Putting his eyebrows up high.

Rick shook his head while tucking in his lips, trying to figure it out while Sean hid behind a display of Hawaiian rolls to hear them better.

Frank leaned on the glass. "That's Bernadette's daughter. Ya know, Larry's girl. Yeah, Bernadette was in here a week ago showing off pictures. She just moved in." He relaxed his face.

Rick looked back between Frank and the path that Loretta took to leave. Sean could feel his face getting hot as he listened.

"And I heard she's single." Frank's eyebrows shot up in the air once again.

Sean couldn't believe what he was hearing. He was stunned for a moment.

"Come on, Frank. That's enough gossip for one day. Just give me a pound of the roasted turkey."

"Look, I'm just telling ya what the word is."

"The word is wrong," Sean barked as he emerged from behind the display case of bread.

Both men turned their attention to the red-faced boy staring at them with daggers. Sean could feel his eyes getting watery from the overload of emotion, but like a reflex, his legs were already running towards the nearest exit.

"Well, that's what I heard from Bennie," Frank admitted with his eyebrows now as high as they could go while pointing to the back room of the deli with his right thumb.

"Just get me the usual, ya troublemaker." Rick turned back, took a deep breath, and went about his business.

Chapter 12

The bad dreams were back. Sean's only comfort now was his running and the Paladin comic books. Coming back from a run one day, Larry called Sean over to the garage.

"Hey, I wanted to show you these." He pulled down a box from a shelf and put it on top of a workbench. "They were my son's." Larry pulled out a few comic books. Sean's eyes went wide with hope. *Maybe it's here. Maybe he has the last edition.* Sean had mixed feelings about finding out how Paladin died. He wanted to have closure, but he didn't want something else to remind him of his father's death. He couldn't help himself and rifled through the box.

"I thought you could be the caretaker for them now."

There were at least forty comics, but only two of them were Paladin and they were only issues three and eight.

Sean blew his breath out hard. "Thanks," he replied as he lifted the box and took it into the house, not waiting for a reaction from Larry.

Vivi was playing with a dollhouse that belonged to Loretta when she was young. Nana B kept almost all the toys from her children's childhood. Sean left the box in a corner by the coat rack.

"Shen, play with me," Vivi called out to him.

Sean didn't want to be mean, so he decided to pretend he couldn't hear her. He started walking up the stairs to his room when he heard Nana B say his name. He already knew that trick wouldn't work with his grandmother, so he froze on the stairs, picturing her wearing a velvet glove.

As Nana B approached, Sean could somehow feel her folding her arms.

"I know you heard your sister."

"I was just feeling tired. I was going to take a nap."

"Well, why don't you let her know that?"

Sean turned around slowly. He stared at Nana B for a moment. She was smiling like she knew the secret to life. And all he had to do was ask, and she would share that secret with him. He came back down the stairs and walked over to his sister. Vivi immediately threw her arms around his leg the instant he was in front of her.

"Shen, you play with me now."

Sean hugged her back. It had been so long since he allowed himself to show or receive love. It was like a man who was starving, finally eating for the first time in weeks. He couldn't hold it down and the food was regurgitated. Sean felt his eyes watering.

Vivi let go of his leg to grab a doll to give to him, but by the time she lifted it up, he was already out the door again. Too quick for Nana B to get a word in. She just stood there fixing her hair from the sudden gust of wind caused by Sean's exit. Walking away to fight the battle another day, she went over to Vivi and kneeled next to her.

"Here Nana B, you be her." She handed her the doll meant for Sean.

Nana B grinned and used her left hand to push Vivi's sandy blonde hair behind her tiny ear. "Be happy to, my dear."

Chapter 13

*T*he week had passed by in a similar fashion. Loretta hadn't felt like much had changed except the scenery. She stood at the stove making scrambled eggs for the kids and Larry. Nana B walked in and took out a bowl from the cabinet.

"I'm making eggs, Mom. You want any?"

"No, Honey. If I don't have my bowl of Fiber Plus, I'm not regular for the rest of the day."

"Okay, got it," Loretta said, trying to not engage any further.

Nana B smiled to herself.

Cartoons and Vivi's laughter could be heard from the other room.

"Where's Sean?" Nana B asked while pouring her cereal.

"You know where he is." Loretta continued to stir the eggs in the pan.

Nana B paused for a second to concentrate on putting the right amount of milk in her bowl. "School begins in seven weeks here." She pulled a spoon from the drawer.

"I know Mom. I'm just not sure he's ready yet."

"Seven weeks is a long time." She placed the spoon in her bowl.

"I don't think it's a good idea to rush him."

"So, you think it would be better if a new student begins in the middle of the school year," Nana B inquired while pulling out a chair to sit at the kitchen table.

Loretta was silent.

"You moved down here to make a different start for the kids."

"Mom, I know. I just don't want to push him."

"You haven't been pushing him," she insisted while stirring her cereal. "Maybe he needs a little push."

Loretta started making the plates. She stuck Sean's in the microwave to keep warm until he got back.

"Vivi, your eggs are ready."

Vivi came running in, laughing while hugging Figaro.

Nana B managed to grab Vivi and sneak in a kiss before she sat down. Then she refocused her attention on Loretta. "Today we're going to swing by the school and register him," Nana B declared plainly.

Loretta set Vivi's and Larry's plates down. As if on cue, Larry walked in and sat at the table.

"Thank you, Loretta."

"No problem, Larry," Loretta said, smiling while avoiding her mother's gaze.

Larry dived into the food.

"It will be good for him. He'll make new friends," Nana B affirmed while Loretta sat next to her.

She grabbed Loretta's wrist gently. "It will help him move on."

Both Larry and Vivi stopped eating.

"Loretta, look at me."

Loretta, reluctantly and without moving her head, pulled her eyes up to her mother.

"It will help you move on." Nana B's voice was confident.

Loretta reflected on her words and swallowed hard. "After breakfast, we can go."

"Good." Nana B shook Loretta's wrist before letting go. "You'll see. I'm right."

"Isn't your cereal getting soggy?" Loretta said as she looked away.

"That's the way I like it." She finally put a spoonful in her mouth.

Vivi looked over at Larry. He gave her a quick wink, letting her know it was safe to eat again.

Chapter 14

Sean was in his new-old room. He found a Yellow Pages phone book in the closet and was skimming for comic book stores. He started writing the names and addresses in the area on a Post-It note pack he had stolen from a kitchen drawer. There was a knock at his door. Without waiting for permission, Nana B was in the doorway.

"Take a walk with me."

"Maybe later."

"I'll meet you downstairs." Her tone didn't change. That was what was so powerful about his grandmother. She got what she wanted without anger. She didn't yell or raise her voice; she didn't even have to change the inflection.

"Grab your jacket. It's windy today," she added before she was gone.

Sean moved the heavy book off his lap. He looked at the open window, contemplating whether or not there was a way out of this.

As if reading his thoughts, Nana B called from downstairs, "Don't keep a lady waiting now."

Sean got up and went to the stairs. Bernadette opened the door and zipped up her coat. She saw that Sean was on his way and decided to wait outside for him. He grabbed his jacket and closed the door behind him.

Nana B took him on a route that he hadn't seen before. He always ran forward from the house. He didn't think to go behind it. The neighborhood was a lot quieter here than back in Staten Island.

"Down this street is Wade K-8 Center. I know you're not excited to start school."

"Not really," Sean responded, staring at the rocks he was kicking.

"Your mom thinks that you should wait to start until you feel ready."

Sean nodded. He didn't actually know his mother's plans, but more time sounded good to him.

"I told her that was a mistake." Sean's head swung up towards her. "That's right. You are already behind from what I hear. Now I know your teachers back home gave you a pass, and it goes without saying why they did." She paused for a second to let that sink in. "But I convinced your mother to register you today. I wanted to tell you this because I don't want you upset with her. She has enough on her plate. This was my idea. And it's a good one. You don't need to fall any more behind." She looked up at the sky. "Plus, you need to get out more."

"I run all the…"

"I know, I know. You run," she interrupted. "That's not you going out, though. That's you staying in." Nana B stopped walking to give Sean her full attention. "Do you understand what I mean?"

Sean knew what he was expected to say but couldn't bring himself to say it. He looked at her and then all around, his eyes unable to focus on anything.

Nana B took a deep breath. "Maybe you don't." She looked in the direction he was staring. "But that's okay. You will one day." She started walking back to the house.

Sean didn't follow her this time.

"If you wanna run, it's okay. I'll meet you back at the house. By the way, your mother is taking you two school shopping next Wednesday for uniforms. They're having a sale."

Sean heard the words as he took off.

Chapter 15

Sean avoided everyone for the next three days. He decided to spend as much time as he could focusing on finding the last issue of Paladin. He continued to research locations for the coveted comic. He decided he would map out all the stores within fifty miles. He found six. Sean would have to ask Larry to take him because he was still trying to evade the attention of the older women in the house. Sean made his way to the garage where Larry always seemed to be when he wasn't in the house.

Larry had his head under a car hood.

"Hey, Larry?"

"Hey, kiddo." Larry took his head out, "Ya need something?"

"Yes." Sean didn't want to seem greedy or ask for too much, so he said, "Do ya think you could take me to three comic book stores today?" He would have to find another way to get to the other three.

"Well, sure." Larry started wiping his hands on an already dirty rag. "Let's take the truck." He pointed to an old beat-up vehicle that Sean thought was there for parts, or as some weird decoration.

Larry grabbed keys off a hook and smiled from ear to ear. Sean forced a smile and followed him.

The car ride was mostly quiet. Sean enjoyed it. The only time Larry spoke was to ask which store they were going to first or next. He kept smiling though, he just seemed happy to spend time with Sean. *He probably gets sick of being around women all the time*, Sean imagined.

*****

They made their way to the first comic store very quickly and left as quickly. Comics R Us was more geared towards the kiddie crowd. Comics, Comics, and More Comics had some issues, but not the one Sean needed. The last store, Virginia Comics, took more time to navigate. Larry and Sean couldn't find anyone who worked there besides the clueless cashier who shrugged his shoulders to any and all of their questions. The two of them wandered the comic book store searching but to no avail. Suddenly, the door swung open and the bells attached jingled, breaking Sean's concentration. He looked up at the mirror that was used for spying on the customers to see who had entered. All Sean could see was an X-Men backpack, well that and Larry's reflection scratching his head. He figured Larry might be getting restless, so he went back to his mission. A few moments went by, then…

"This is him. He's trying to find Paladin comics."

Sean turned his head and did a double-take. He assumed the figure in the mirror was a boy, but there she stood. She had long jet-black hair that was in a front braid. One of her farrow-shaped eyes was somewhat covered by her hair, but Sean could still see that it was a different color from the other. One dark brown and the other hazel with streaks of yellow.

"Hi, Sean." She pushed her long-sleeved shirt up on one side, just enough to expose her hand, which she now held out.

Sean started feeling light-headed. He felt his face getting hot and his hands getting sweaty.

"Well, don't be shy. Shake Ondrea's hand."

The sound of Larry's voice helped Sean refocus and realize that he had forgotten to breathe. He took a long, deep breath and raised his right arm. When their hands met, Sean swore he felt electricity in his veins.

"Ondrea," he whispered, staring at her wildly, with wide eyes. Three freckles laid at the top of the bridge of her nose. One deep dark eye and the other resembling a sunflower to Sean. Both surrounded by long eyelashes.

"Sean," she whispered back, smiling, then looked up at Larry for guidance.

"So, do ya have any tips for us?" Larry shifted his weight and placed his left hand on Sean's right shoulder, giving a subtle cue to let go of her hand.

Sean finally let go and out of embarrassment stared at the floor.

"I would say call the store ahead of time, so ya don't waste your time or gas." Her voice was confident.

At the obvious advice, Sean felt silly and continued to stare at the floor which looked like it hadn't been vacuumed in months. There was an old piece of gum on it not too far from his sneakers.

"I can try to call also. See what I find out."

"Ondrea here is the go-to girl of the neighborhood. She knows everything that goes on in this neck of the woods." Larry gestured for Sean to look up.

Sean nodded but kept his eyes in place.

"Well, I should go. My dad only gave me an hour to look around."

"Okay, sweetheart. Sean and I will see ya around I'm sure," Larry said, grinning.

"Oh, I'm sure I'll run into you sometime."

At the word "run" Sean looked up and saw Ondrea wearing a small simper upon her face. Ondrea walked away, but before she went down an aisle she looked back at Sean and smiled again. Sean returned the smile and felt dizzy.

"We should be getting back, too. Otherwise, your Nana will have my head."

Sean was still beaming as they left the store.

*****

When they returned home, Sean was still dazed by the whole Ondrea encounter. He got out of the car and stared up at the sky. It was almost sundown. He took a deep breath with his eyes closed, taking in the air and holding it. Then he looked over at Larry who was wearing a coy look.

"What?"

"You know what," Larry responded coolly while walking up to the house. He waited a moment on the porch for Sean and then finally said, "Ya coming or what, lover boy?"

Sean blushed at the name and turned away from the house.

"Alright, I'll tell them to keep your plate warm." Larry walked inside.

Sean took another deep breath and went for a run. This run was different from all the others, though. The air, the road, his legs all felt different.

Chapter 16

$\mathcal{S}$ean didn't know how long he ran, just that he ran long enough to feel fatigued. He slowed down to a light jog when he heard a loud noise. He heard it again and again. Sean stopped to try to identify it. He realized that it was a chopping sound.

It was coming from one of the backyards. Sean was not usually a nosy kid, but there was something strange about the noise. *It was happening too fast. How could it be happening so fast? Must be some machine.* He started walking closer to the source of the sound. His curiosity led him to peek through a crack in a red-painted wood fence. There was a man inside who had his back to Sean. He was wearing a white tank top and had long brown hair. Long for a man was Sean's opinion anyway. He moved to a different angle to see more. The ax was going up and down. Again and again. Picking up wood and chopping it. Again and again. Sean's eyes grew with astonishment. The man was the machine. Sean shifted his weight back to see the man again. This time he focused mainly on what was behind the man, which was a pile of wood almost as high as the fence, which had to be at least six feet tall. Sean was in such disbelief that he didn't notice how quiet it had suddenly become.

The man still had his back to him but turned his head to the left. "Enjoying the show?"

Sean froze. *How could he have heard me?* Sean looked at the ground and realized that a small thin tree branch under his shoe had given him away. *Wait. That voice.* Sean knew that voice. His brain was scrambling. He looked up to see Rick staring at the crack in the fence. Sean jumped backwards as a reflex and slammed into a large sycamore tree.

"You spying on me or something" Rick climbed up the fence to get a better look at his Peeping Tom. He was wearing the same pair of glasses from the other day.

"I'm not," Sean quickly replied.

"Hey, I remember you." Rick's demeanor suddenly changed.

Sean shook his head.

"From Shop 'N Save."

Sean was sweating more than Rick now.

"I wanted to talk to you."

Sean slid his back across the tree.

"Hey, Rick," a voice called from across the street.

"Afternoon, Mrs. Quinn."

Sean didn't even look back; he took the opportunity and flew down the street, taking the first corner he could to get out of sight.

"How's your day going?" Rick said to Mrs. Quinn while watching Sean disappear.

Sean leaned against a wall waiting for his heart rate to slow down. He felt foolish thinking that Rick would have chased after him. Once his breath was caught, he walked the rest of the way home, which gave him time to reflect.

Chapter 17

The next day Loretta took Sean and Vivi uniform shopping. Sean was starting sixth grade and Vivi was going into a VPK program at Wade K-8 Center. Sean was still in a haze, playing yesterday's events over and over. *Why would that guy need to talk to me? Is Ondrea going into sixth grade also? Why does that guy need so much firewood in the summer? Does Ondrea go to Wade?*

The time, store, and clothes flew by without any other thoughts until Sean spotted a comic book stand across from the uniform store in the mall. He looked over to his mother who was already giving him the okay nod while she zipped up a jacket Vivi was trying on. Sean made his way over to the stand.

Again, disappointment was all he found, but the teenage girl behind the stand must have felt sorry for Sean because she said, "Tell me whatcha looking for and I'll tell ya where to find it."

Sean looked up to see a Hispanic girl with thin eyebrows and long black hair covered in blonde highlights in a fishtail braid. She had deep dark eyes. *Ondrea has one dark eye,* Sean thought to himself. Her name tag said "Ava."

"Paladin."

Ava gave one slow nod that seemed to say "of course."

She pressed a button on the register and receipt paper rose. She ripped it off, grabbed a pen from the counter, and began scribbling. Sean waited patiently as she finished and handed him the paper.

"This store has a section dedicated to Paladin. That's the address. It's a bit of a drive but I guarantee you'll find whatcha lookin' for."

As though he held the golden ticket, Sean stared at the paper in amazement.

He didn't have to force a smile when he looked up at Ava. She returned the expression to him, confirming a comradery that was now established.

Chapter 18

When they got home, Sean jumped on the phone and dialed the number on the receipt. The man who answered was very courteous. Sean almost jumped in the air when he learned they had the last edition. The store was over an hour's drive away. Sean was contemplating which adult to ask when he heard Larry calling him.

Sean walked outside. Larry was in the car waiting.

"Hey, wanna take a ride to the hardware store with me?"

"Sure." He jumped into the car. "And maybe we can stop at a comic book store, too?"

Larry put the car into drive. "I don't see why not."

There was silence for some time until Larry politely asked, "So what did ya think of the comics I gave you?"

Sean didn't want to admit that he never looked at any. He didn't even know who put them in his room after he left them at the bottom of the stairs. Already feeling guilty and not wanting to hurt Larry's feelings he answered, "They're good." Sean prayed that would be the end of the conversation because he couldn't remember any of the comics in the box. His prayers were not answered.

"Which one did ya like the most?" Larry gave a genuine smile of curiosity.

Sean quickly scanned his brain. Remembering Ondrea's bookbag, he blurted out, "X-Men."

"Oh, I liked those too."

Sean was thankful for the luck in his guess. It's better to lie in this moment and the moments when his grandmother asked if her cookies were better than Chips Ahoy.

At the store, Larry was perusing the different screwdrivers. "The kind of screwdriver we need is a flathead." Larry picked one up. "Like this one."

Sean nodded as Larry ran his index finger along the top part of the tool.

Suddenly two men walked in and stared in Larry's direction.

"Can't go anywhere without seeing one," one said to the other. "I remember when they wouldn't even come to this part of town."

"They knew their place back then," the other man responded, sucking on the side of his lip.

Sean was thrown back by the comments. He wondered if they bothered Larry. If it did, he didn't let on.

Then Rick walked in. Sean instantly had a theory that Rick was secretly following him, but quickly dismissed it. Sean threw his head down to avoid eye contact and pretended like he was engulfed in the amazement of the screwdrivers before him, but Larry soon foiled this plan.

"Hey, Rick. Have ya met my sidekick here, Sean?"

Before he knew it, Rick was standing right in front of him. He had his trademark sunglasses on as usual. "I've had the pleasure, yes." Rick and Larry shook hands.

Rick turned his head toward the men, who were still whispering and snickering. Sean couldn't make out what they were saying, but he knew the jokes were at Larry's expense. Rick must have had the same thought because his face began to harden.

Larry was, as Sean could remember, the nicest of Nana B's boyfriends. Now that Sean thought about it, he was the only one he could remember, but that didn't change the fact that he was still an incredibly nice guy. That Larry was black didn't matter to anyone in the family. Sean couldn't remember anyone even mentioning it in any capacity. Everyone would just say Nana B's beau when speaking about Larry.

Rick continued to flex his jawbone as he stared at the men. The men must have felt the daggers in their backs, even with Rick's sunglasses on, because they both turned to face him and abruptly stopped laughing. After an uncomfortable moment, both men turned back around, red in the face like two schoolboys who had been caught talking by their teacher.

"Oh, don't mind them, Rick. I never do."

Rick let his face soften again. "You're a smart man, Larry."

Sean couldn't believe it. He would be lying if he said he wasn't impressed. Those men were obviously afraid of Rick. It made sense. It couldn't be denied that Rick was intimidating.

While Larry and Rick discussed tools, Sean used the opportunity to get a good look at him up close. Sean already knew that he was tall, but at the short distance between them, he seemed like a giant. He tried to compare Rick to Leo. After Sean's growth spur, he was the height of Leo's shoulders, but here he only came up to the top of Rick's ribs. And the rest of his body was proportionate to his height, unlike Leo's. The muscles in his shirt looked like they were trying to break free. Sean couldn't help but look at his own arms in comparison. *Is he too broke to buy clothes that actually fit him*? Sean wondered, annoyed. He was still perturbed by the comments made by that deli guy and Rick from the other day.

"Well, I just came in to get a new hammer. My other one broke." Rick reached up to grab the tool with what Sean would describe as a baseball mitt. His hands looked twice as big as Larry's and even bigger than his father's.

Sean was winding up to start running when he heard Larry's words.

"See ya for dinner tonight then."

Sean's mouth dropped open. *What did I miss?* He felt his heart beginning to race.

"That's a good guy there, Sean." Larry rubbed Sean's hair. "He reminds me of..."

Sean was gearing up again to run when he saw Larry's face. He looked sad, sadder than Sean had ever seen him before. He couldn't understand why though. The sight had caused the adrenaline in Sean's veins to subside. He no longer felt the need to run, for the moment.

Chapter 19

After paying for a screwdriver, Larry drove straight home. Sean decided not to remind him about the comic book store that was an hour away. The car ride back home was completely silent. But it was a different silence from their last ride together. Larry didn't look at Sean. He didn't even look toward the road it seemed. It was as if autopilot had taken over and Larry was miles away. He turned when he was supposed to and stopped when he had to, but Larry was not there.

When they pulled up to the driveway. Everyone was waiting for them on the porch. Loretta was reading *Ferdinand the Bull* to Vivi while Nana B was feeding a stray cat.

"Welcome back boys." Nana B was smiling until she saw the look on Larry's face.

"I'm gonna do some work in the garage, Love." He kissed her on the cheek and headed towards his fortress.

"You need me to getcha anything?" Her eyes were filled with concern.

"No, Bernie. Just need to do some work," he reiterated as he continued on his path.

Nana B looked over to Loretta, who had stopped reading and shared the same look of concern.

"Everything alright, mom?" she asked as Vivi got off her lap.

"It will be. He just needs some time alone for a bit," Nana B replied as she watched Vivi pet the cat. "He gets like this sometimes when… you know." They exchanged another look that Sean knew meant something important.

After a short pause, Loretta inquired, "Where did you boys go?"

"Hardware store," Sean mumbled as he walked up the porch, stopping on the middle step.

"Anything interesting happen while you were out?"

Sean couldn't tell whether Nana B was casually asking or whether she was trying to figure out what had triggered Larry.

Sean reflected for a moment and then answered, "We saw Rick."

"Who's Rick?" his mother asked, more to Nana B than to him.

Sean was secretly happy that she didn't remember him.

"The man that lives three streets down. He's the one I told ya about." Nana B gave another look to her daughter, but Loretta just rolled her eyes in response this time.

Vivi came up to Sean with a calico cat in her hands. She was holding the stray in such an awkward childlike manner that the cat began to whine.

"This is Lilly."

Sean picked up the cat from her. "Vivi, this is how you should hold her."

Vivi beamed as she pet the feline. "I love her."

Sean could not help but give a small smile to his sister.

"So, about Rick?" Nana B continued her line of questioning.

Sean suddenly remembered that Rick was coming over for dinner that night. The cat must have sensed Sean's anxiety because she jumped out of his arms and ran behind the house, with Vivi chasing after her.

Nana B and Loretta turned their heads toward the show and then back the other way when they heard Sean's sneakers running in the opposite direction.

Chapter 20

As Sean was running, he realized that he was heading towards Rick's house. He quickly turned the next corner to avoid another confrontation. As he turned, he slammed into something hard that knocked him off his feet. Sean laid there for a moment in pain staring at the clouds.

"Ow! What the hell!"

Sean recognized the voice instantly. He pushed himself up to a sitting position. And there she was rubbing her head leaning on her left side.

"Don't you look where ya running?"

"I'm sorry." Sean leaned on his knees to check her wounds. "Are you bleeding?"

Ondrea moved her hand from her head to inspect. "No, no blood. Just an egg on my forehead." She went back to rubbing her bump.

"I'm so..."

"It's okay," she interrupted him. "Just help me up."

Sean got to his feet and then helped Ondrea to hers.

"I'll live," she mumbled.

Sean felt awful. He started to look off into the distance as she dusted off her light blue jeans.

He felt the same familiar need to escape, the adrenaline coursing through his body. He was about to take off when he felt her grab his shoulder.

"Hey, don't run off on me now Maniac Magee." She pulled him to face her.

Her touch didn't stop the adrenaline. He managed to force out what sounded like "Who?"

"Ya just gonna leave me here hurt?"

He shook his head.

"Sean, right?"

He nodded.

"The quiet kind, huh?"

Sean swallowed hard and forced out, "Ondrea."

"That's right. So, you just moved in like two weeks ago?"

They started walking off together.

"About two weeks," Sean mumbled, but he still couldn't make eye contact, not for more than a couple of seconds at a time, anyway.

"Hey, I'm sorry." He pointed with his chin to the now visible bump on her head.

"I know you are." Ondrea gave him a small smile. She retrieved a gray hat from her X-Men backpack. She pulled it over her head, specifically hiding the bump. "Don't worry about it. You'll make it up to me."

Sean nodded then looked at her for further instructions. He watched as Ondrea placed her hands firmly on the straps of her backpack. Her knuckles were covered by the sleeves of her long red shirt.

"You can start by showing me your comic book collection. I figure you gotta have one since I saw you and Larry at Virginia Comics."

"It's mainly Paladin."

"That's okay. I love Paladin. He's not my ultimate favorite, but he makes the top ten."

Sean's eyes gleamed at the thought of having something in common with her.

They approached the house. Ondrea seemed to feel right at home as she walked ahead of him.

"Shen, who's this?" Vivi asked as she grabbed Ondrea's hand.

"Oh my God, is this your sister?" Ondrea squatted down to meet her eye level.

"Yes, her name's Viviana, but everyone calls her Vivi."

"She is too cute." Ondrea held her little hand up to her own. Vivi grabbed her hand again and led her to the dollhouse.

"Here, you be her." She handed her a doll with black hair.

"Let me get you some ice." Sean went to the kitchen.

"Sean, is that you?" Loretta walked in with a load of laundry. "Oh, hello."

"Hi, I'm Sean's friend Ondrea." She stood up holding the doll Vivi gave her.

Loretta placed the basket down on the couch. "Oh, Sean's friend," she said, with a grin now on her face. "It's nice to meet you. I'm his mother, Loretta."

They shook hands as Sean came back with some ice.

"Sean, you didn't tell me," Loretta stopped herself, realizing she may embarrass him. "What's the ice for?"

"I..."

Ondrea intervened, "I fell outside, and your son was nice enough to offer me some aid." She took the ice from Sean.

"Well, I guess you fell into my son." She gestured towards the bump now appearing on Sean's head. "Running?" She looked to Ondrea for confirmation.

Ondrea smiled and looked at the floor.

"That's what I thought." She shook her head at Sean.

"Shen got hurt," Vivi said as she pointed to Sean's forehead.

Loretta walked over to Sean and examined the swelling. After checking on her son she made her way over to Ondrea and asked, "Are you okay?"

"I'm fine." Ondrea handed the ice back to Sean. "We can share."

"She's a tough cookie," Nana B announced as she walked in.

"Hi, Ms. Del Luca."

Nana B clicked her tongue. "Bernadette," she insisted as she gave Ondrea a big hug. "So, what are you kids up to besides getting hurt today?" She still held Ondrea in an embrace.

"Sean was going to show me his comics."

Nana B finally released Ondrea, who seemed relieved and sad at the same time. "Oh good. I placed a box full of comics in his room the other day."

Sean blushed when he felt Bernadette's eyes on him. Ondrea gave the doll back to Vivi and walked over to Nana B, who kept her eyes on Sean.

"Awesome, why don't cha show me?"

"You guys are going upstairs?" Loretta asked.

"They'll be fine, Loretta." Nana B walked over to him and put her hand on his shoulder. "Doors stay open when you have girls over," she whispered into his ear.

Sean's eyes met hers and he knew that there would be a talk later.

"Let me know if you guys need anything," Loretta said as Sean led Ondrea up the stairs, handing back the ice.

"But, what about my dolls!" Vivi cried out running to Ondrea.

"I promise to play with you before I leave." She put out her right hand to show her pinky. "Pinky promise."

Vivi put out hers to tie them. "Pinky promise," she echoed as she hugged Ondrea before running back to her dollhouse.

*****

"Wow, still unpacking, huh?" Ondrea asked, looking around Sean's bare room.

It was true Sean didn't have the energy or patience or care to set up his room.

Sean cleared his throat, responding with, "Work in progress."

"Nice posters," Ondrea commented on the Black Panther and Spiderman graphics hung up behind the bed.

"Uh, they're not mine. This was Larry's son's old room," Sean admitted.

"Still nice." Ondrea laid the ice in a bowl that had been forgotten about from the day before on the nightstand. "You have some cool comics in here." She wiped her hands over her jeans to dry them and began to rummage through the box. "Superman, X-Men, Captain America."

Sean opened a drawer from the nightstand to take out his Paladin comics.

He gently placed them down between them on the bed.

Ondrea's pupils grew in size as she ran her fingers through the pile. "You have editions one through twelve?" she accused excitedly.

"Just need one more."

"Do you know how much these are worth?"

"Not as much as the last one I'm guessing." Sean felt more at ease with her now.

Ondrea opened her backpack and took out two comics. There were both Catwoman is-sues. "I always carry one or two with me. She's my absolute favorite." She handed them to Sean to look over.

He flipped through the pages. "Why is she your favorite?"

Ondrea shrugged her shoulders. "She's tough… ya know." She began to stare into space. "She does what she wants and doesn't let anyone hurt her."

Sean turned his head towards her. *She looks sad, but still beautiful*, Sean mused. He scanned his brain to think of something to say. "Can I borrow this to read?"

Ondrea snapped out of her own head. "Of course, just be careful," she reminded him. Once again, she looked happy.

"Well, I already know your favorite. You wanna tell me why?"

Sean grinned.

Ondrea gently nudged him, "Hey, you started this."

"I don't know. I guess he has all these flaws. Ya know. He seems to get tired of saving people. Like he wants to live his own life." He picked up a Paladin comic. "He just seems like he could be real, ya know."

Sean was honest, but he felt silly about what he had just admitted. He was sure he'd blown it with Ondrea with his childish ideas until she replied, "I get it. He's like the guy who lives down the street or your next-door neighbor, just with some awesome powers. I think that might be his hamartia. He wants to be like everyone else."

"His what?"

"Hamartia. The flaw that leads to the downfall of a hero. Ya know, like Superman always must do the right thing. Or Iron Man's pride."

"Wow, you know a lot about this stuff." He stared in awe of her.

She looked away humbly and remarked, "That's just Superhero 101. Hey, did you know Paladin is left-handed?"

Sean shook his head in disbelief.

"Yeah, just look at the graphics." She opened issue five, *Paladin vs Alois: Friend or Foe*, "See here. When he grabs his staff." She pointed to another picture. "And here when he just holds it. You can look through all your comics to see."

Sean was in amazement. He gazed at the images for some time before moving his stare back to her. He looked back and forth between each of her eyes trying to figure out which one he liked more.

"*Knock. Knock,*" Loretta spoke the words while softly knocking on the open door. "Hey, don't wanna interrupt you guys, but we were wondering if maybe Ondrea wanted to stay for dinner."

"I'd love to. As long as I'm home before eight," said Ondrea.

Sean smiled from ear to ear.

"Great, so seven of us then."

"Seven?" Sean questioned.

"Larry told us his friend is coming also," Loretta answered.

Sean's expression slowly diminished as he realized who the seventh person was. "Rick," he grumbled.

"Rick Neige?" Ondrea asked eagerly.

"I'm not sure about the last name," said Loretta.

"Tall, tan, muscles."

"That's him," Nana B called out from the other room.

Loretta put up both eyebrows as she shook her head and then said, "Okay, so we'll call you when it's time to help." She pointed to Sean.

"I'll help, too."

"Nonsense, you're our guest."

"I want to, though," Ondrea insisted.

"That's sweet of you. I'll let you two get back to the comics for now." She left as quietly as she came.

Meanwhile, Sean's brain was swimming.

Ondrea noticed. "Is everything alright?"

"Sure." He forced himself to lie.

"You don't like Rick?"

Sean snapped his head around to her. *Am I that obvious or is she just that good at reading me?*

"It makes sense. To me anyway." Ondrea was speaking casually. "Rick is some guy that might get close to your mom. Some guy who isn't your dad." She spoke more sincerely now. "I'm sorry about your dad."

Once again, Sean was surprised. Ondrea squinted her eyes. "Small town."

"It's okay." Sean stared out his window, just past her shoulder. He didn't have the urge to run. Ondrea had mentioned his father and he wasn't running. This was new terrain for Sean.

Chapter 21

Sean and Ondrea were setting up the table together while Larry, who was in better spirits, was bringing two extra chairs out to the dining room. Loretta and Nana B were finishing up the last touches on dinner. Mashed potatoes, green beans, salad, oven-baked rolls, and pork roast. Vivi came running over and stole Ondrea away. Sean and Larry carried the dishes over to the table, while the ladies brought out pitchers of lemonade and water. A loud knock at the door startled Sean so much so that he almost dropped the green beans.

"That must be Rick. I'll get it." Larry hurried over to the front door.

"Ya alright?" Loretta asked Sean who just nodded quickly. "You should sit next to Ondrea at the table."

Sean nodded again, this time slowly.

"Hope I'm not late." Rick walked in holding some kind of pie.

Larry took it from him and brought it into the kitchen saying, "You're just in time."

Rick didn't have his hat or his reflective sunglasses on. He looked so different that Sean almost didn't recognize him.

"You must be Rick. I'm Loretta." She walked around Sean to shake his hand.

"Nice to meet you."

"My mother tells me you live a couple of streets over from us."

"That's correct, ma'am."

"I don't ever remember seeing you."

Again, Sean felt a bit of satisfaction in the fact that Rick had not left a lasting impression upon his mother from that time in the grocery store.

"Well, I think it was your boy who I've run into before." Rick signaled with his head towards Sean.

"That seems to be how everyone meets Sean," Ondrea chimed in as she walked into the room with Vivi.

"That certainly sounds like him," Loretta said, smiling.

"Hey, Rick." Ondrea sat down.

"Hey, Dre."

Questions swirled around in Sean's head. *Dre? He has a nickname for her. Am I the only person that doesn't like this guy? Is Ondrea right? Is it only because of my mom?*

At that moment, Nana B walked in with the napkins, and Larry followed behind her. She handed the napkins to Loretta.

"Rick, I always forget how long your hair is." Bernadette gave him a kiss on the cheek.

"Well, when I wear my hat it's misleading."

"Sit," Nana B said, pointing to the chair next to him. "Let's start this feast shall we." She sat next to Larry towards the other end of the table.

Sean looked around, suddenly realizing there were only three seats left. One next to Rick and the other two on both sides of Ondrea. His mother hadn't sat down yet, but she had just finished handing out the napkins, and Rick got up to pull out the chair next to him for her. Sean leaped into it.

"Oh." Loretta looked over to Ondrea and back to Sean. "You're sitting here?"

"Yes, I am sitting here," Sean stated sternly.

Rick let go of the chair and returned to his seat, with an awkward grin.

Loretta sat down next to Ondrea, and they exchanged smiles. Vivi hopped onto the other chair and was thrilled to sit next to Ondrea.

Nana B announced, "Just a quick prayer before we begin."

Everyone reached out to hold the person's hand next to them. Sean was reluctant to hold Rick's, but after an earnest look from Nana B, he grabbed it.

While the others had their heads down, Sean had his up, watching Rick intensely. *No, it's not just about Mom. Something about this guy doesn't add up.* Sean was so fixated on his target that he didn't hear Nana B finish the prayer. When everyone raised their heads, Rick must have felt Sean's daggers because he looked directly at him. Dark green eyes were peering back into Sean's. *Eyes of a villain*, Sean surmised.

Rick grinned politely at him. An expression Sean did not return as he pulled his hand away.

Most of the dinner was a blur, topics like sports, school starting, and the best restaurants in town were discussed.

Sean spent most of the time keeping an eye on Rick to make sure he didn't get too comfortable talking to his mother. Ondrea, on more than one occasion, tried to start a conversation with Sean, but he was too preoccupied with what he felt was his duty. Additionally, Vivi was pining for Ondrea's attention whenever it wasn't given.

Sean was happy when everyone got up to put their plates away. He lunged at Rick's to keep him seated, plus he figured he might win some brownie points with Nana B for being so "gracious" to the company.

When Sean came back out from putting the plates away, he was sure everyone would say their goodbyes. He didn't want to see Ondrea go, but it was the sacrifice he would have to make for now. To his disappointment, he had forgotten about the pie. Larry came out from behind him holding it. Sean swore in his head as he returned to his seat. Loretta began handing out pieces and asked Rick how much he wanted.

"Just a sliver for me. Dinner was delicious and filling." He smiled.

She smiled back and Sean grumbled under his breath.

"Sean, how big of a piece do you want?"

"I don't want any."

Loretta, with a puzzled face, questioned, "But you love apple pie."

With a deep breath in, he muttered, "Not anymore."

"Wow, so many changes," she said, giving a small piece to Vivi.

"Yes, a lot of changes," he sneered as he looked up at her. Sean immediately regretted his words and tone after he saw the hurt look his mother wore.

Larry switched the subject to lighten the tension. "Hey Rick, you remember that time Mr. Rogers' car broke down?"

Rick nodded while still chewing on the pie.

"I tell you kids. This man single-handedly moved that car across the highway. And not one of those newer mini cars either. It was a truck like mine."

Rick wiped his mouth with a napkin. "I recall you were there helping as well."

"No sir, I got there after the fact. Got to see the end of the show, though. I mean you didn't even struggle a little. Not even a bead of sweat on ya."

Rick raised his eyebrows and said humbly, "Guess I just had some adrenaline in my blood that day."

Sean pictured the event in his head, but still had the nagging feeling of guilt. He looked over at his mother. Sean could tell she was forcing a happy expression on her face. She wasn't even eating her slice of pie, only moving her fork around it.

"Maybe it was from your accident." Larry pointed at Rick.

Nana B lightly hit Larry with her elbow.

"What? Sometimes people go into comas, and something changes in them. I read about it somewhere, Bernie."

"Did you ever think that maybe that might be a touchy subject for Rick?" Nana B tried to say quietly, but it was more like a stage whisper.

Coma? Sean's head was spinning. His undivided attention was now on this conversation.

"What's a coma," Vivi asked, with pie smeared across her face.

"It's okay Bernadette. A coma is what happens sometimes to someone who gets badly hurt in the head. Truly I don't remember much of it."

"Someone tried to hurt you?" Vivi's voice sounded scared.

He looked over to Vivi and tried to reassure her. "No, I don't think anyone was trying to hurt me."

"You're the only person I've ever met that has been in a coma," Ondrea said. And everyone else agreed.

"Coma, that's pretty serious," Loretta remarked. The current topic had distracted her as well.

"Yeah, I suppose. Like I said, I don't remember much about it. Only what happened after I woke up."

Ondrea suddenly sprang up. "Is that the right time?" She was pointing to the grandfather clock in the corner of the room. "Is it eight-fifteen?"

"I think it's a bit slow." Larry checked his watch.

"I have to go, or my father will be mad." She ran over to her backpack and made her way to the door.

"Let Larry drive you, Honey." Nana B was now up and walking towards her.

"I can drive you, Dre." Rick stood up.

"No, no, please. Thanks for dinner and everything... I gotta go. Bye, everyone."

Vivi rushed over to her. "Don't go, no..."

Ondrea gave her a quick hug. "I promise I'll come over and play with you soon."

"Pinky promise?"

"Pinky promise," Ondrea repeated as she twisted her pinky around Vivi's. She gave another quick wave before running out. "Bye, everyone."

"Hopefully, Cinderella doesn't lose a sneaker." Nana B was watching her race down the street from the window. "You guys have a lot in common, huh Sean." She patted him on the shoulder as she passed to get back to her seat.

Sean felt so bad about Ondrea and his mother that he couldn't even enjoy the sight of Rick leaving, which was soon after Ondrea's great escape. At the door, while saying his thanks and goodbyes, no one questioned when Rick requested to have Sean walk him out, no one except Sean.

Sean wracked his brain as he followed him out the door. *What does this guy want? What is his plan? Does he think he can scare me?*

"Hey, I just wanted to apologize for the other day."

Sean was stunned at hearing those words.

"I get it. Ya know. That's your mom and it's one of your jobs to protect her. I didn't mean any harm talking about her. And I want you to know that you don't have to worry about me."

"I wasn't worried," Sean responded coolly.

Rick nodded and tucked his lips into his mouth before he said, "Okay then, so we good?"

Sean nodded back, but without eye contact.

"Can we shake on it?"

Sean put his hand out and they shook. He watched Rick drive off in his pick-up truck and even though he got the confirmation he deeply desired, he still had a weird feeling when it came to Rick. If he was being honest to himself, he wasn't sure if the feeling was completely bad.

Chapter 22

After dinner, Sean went to his room for a while replaying the day's events in his mind. He couldn't sleep so he went for a run to clear his head. When he got back, he saw his mother on the porch sitting by herself. He knew somehow that she wasn't just waiting up for him. Loretta was silent as he walked over to her.

Sean decided to speak first. He blurted out, "I'm sorry."

"What are you sorry for?" She still wasn't making eye contact.

"I don't know." He sat on the top of the porch step. "I'm just sorry."

"I wanna ask you something." She finally looked at him. Her eyes were glassy.

Sean wanted to go and run again but his legs were sore, so he just turned away from her.

"Are you happy we moved here?" She entreated him for an honest answer. Before Sean could even think of what to say his mother continued. "I know it's only been two weeks, but I had sort of an epiphany while you were out there." She paused as if she was trying to find the strength to say the next words. "I realized that I didn't even ask you if you were okay with moving here." She let out a long breath. "For that, I'm the one who should be sorry."

Sean turned and his eyes met hers. He could see the tears getting ready to fall. He wasn't used to her showing so much emotion. He had only seen her cry twice that he remembered. Both happened around two years ago. Sean didn't like the feeling it gave him. He wanted to escape. He stood up, clenched his fists, and closed his eyes tightly. It took all of his effort not to move. He swallowed hard, opened his eyes, and said, "I like it here."

Loretta smiled so abruptly that the tears fell down her cheeks. She quickly wiped them away. "Really?"

"I mean so far."

Loretta stood up and moved to the chair next to where he was standing. She grabbed his hand and asked, "You're not just saying that?"

"I mean I haven't started school yet but–yeah, I do. I like it here."

She pulled him into her, throwing her arms around him. "I'm so glad. I was so afraid that I'd made a grave mistake. I just… I just want to make the right decisions for you and Vivi."

"I know mom." He pried himself free from her. "I'm going to bed now."

"I'm going to stay out here a little longer," Loretta said as she stared up at the sky painted with stars

Sean stood by the door. He knew he should hug or kiss her, or show any kind of affection to his mother, but he couldn't bring himself to do it. Not yet. So, he turned around and went inside the house.

Chapter 23

*T*hat night Sean had a strange dream. Ondrea was walking across the street to get to him. She was smiling and waving. It made Sean's heart swell in his chest. He couldn't take his eyes off of her until a loud noise pulled his attention away. A truck was racing down the road and was about to hit Ondrea. Sean tried with his might to run. He pushed himself like never before, but his legs felt heavy. He struggled to move them. The more effort he used the heavier they became. Sean was not fast enough. The truck rushed past him. He could do nothing now but watch the carnage. Ondrea froze. In that instant, out of nowhere, Rick appeared in front of the truck to save her. He used his body as a shield. Sean heard the crash and then only his own breathing. He woke up grabbing the sides of his bed for security. He took a deep breath and got up to get a glass of water. Sean played the dream back repeatedly in his head. It suddenly occurred to him that the dream wasn't about his father. He tried to pinpoint the day that the nightmares had stopped and the reason or reasons why. Was it the day he met Ondrea? Was it because of her or because of Rick? Maybe both. Sean couldn't be sure, but the nightmares had stopped. It was all bittersweet to him. His dad being there with him, with his mom and sister, just being there. These dreams were nightmares to him because of the pain that came once he woke- -and Sean was there, and his father was not. It was in every one of those moments that he had to realize all over again that his dad was gone. It felt like losing him every day, every night, every time he woke up.

It was three o'clock in the morning. Sean knew that his mother would not be happy with him going out so late, or maybe so early. He rationalized it to himself by saying, *this is a safe neighborhood. I have reflective shoes. This is a quiet town. I run in the bicycle lanes. Everyone else is probably asleep.* He finished tying his shoes and quietly snuck out of the house. He ran slowly at first, warming up his legs. *I'll run by Rick's house and circle around*, he told himself. Nothing much going on at Rick's. The lights were out. Sean continued down the street. Every house had its lights off except one. This particular house had two lights on.

One downstairs and the other upstairs. He slowed his pace to a slow jog and eventually a full stop.

Sean was suddenly startled by the sound of a man yelling. He tried to slow his heart rate down but jumped again as a cat scurried under a parked car. Once Sean calmed his nerves he looked around to ensure that no one would see him as he walked over to the house. He stealthily crept up the outside stairs and crouched down as he made his way to the closest window. He peered inside, unable to ignore his curiosity. A man was lying on a couch watching television. The lights of the screen periodically shined upon his face. Sean was able to make out some details of the man. He had a five o'clock shadow that reached from the bottom of his neck up to almost the top of his cheeks. His nose was slender like Ondrea's but much longer. He had dark black hair that also resembled hers.

Suddenly the man jerked up to a sitting position and roared, "I said stay in your room!"

Sean couldn't hear the voice of the other person or even see their presence, but he felt that it was Ondrea.

"I don't care if you're thirsty. You should've thought about that before you broke the rules. You'll get something to drink when I say ya good and ready. Do you understand?" He paused for a moment and then stood up. "Do I have to come up there?! I said do you understand me!" He laid back down on the couch and grumbled to himself, "Selfish like your mother."

Sean stepped away from the window and gazed up to what had to be Ondrea's room. He could see her silhouette draped on the curtain. She was sitting by the window with her legs up to her chest and her head resting against her knees. He was going to call up to her but stopped himself.

On a sprint, he was home again. He raced to the kitchen and grabbed a bottle of water from the fridge. In a flash, he was back in front of her house, climbing up a tree that wasn't exactly close to her window. He doubted his ability for a moment but reminded himself that he was a pretty decent pitcher on the baseball team. After all, before he'd quit the team, Sean was the backup for Tim. And everyone said Tim would play in the major leagues one day. Maybe even for the Yankees. He managed to toss the bottle near her window. Once his feet were on the ground again, he hid behind a nearby car. Sean watched as she opened her window and examined the bottle. She peered around the street for a moment, back and forth, before closing her window. Sean did not stay to see whether or not she drank from the bottle. He hoped she would. He hoped that he could do more for her. For Ondrea, he hoped for a lot.

Chapter 24

Sean never made it back to his room that night. He slept on the couch and was awakened by a pulling and tugging on his shirt. Lilly was kneading on his chest. Then he heard Vivi giggling.

"She loves you, Shen."

"I can see that." He sat up which made the cat jump off of him and onto the carpet. She licked her left paw before walking away with Vivi following eagerly.

Sean stood up and grabbed the comic book from the coffee table next to the couch. He had been reading Ondrea's Catwoman, *Metamorphosis* before he passed out. It made him feel close to her. When he opened it to see how far he had gotten, the piece of paper he was using as a bookmark fell out. Sean picked it up from the floor. It was the receipt paper from Ava at the comic stand. It read Irruption Comics. The name of the store with the Paladin section. Sean had forgotten about it with all the events going on. He decided it would be the best distraction from the guilt he felt about Ondrea. Sean jumped in and out of the shower, grabbed a granola bar, checked the bus schedule, and made his way out the door.

Sean used some of his birthday money for the bus ride. He hadn't touched it at all. He had the wad of two hundred and twelve dollars in the pocket of his shorts, ready to be spent on Paladin if needed. He let his mind wander, as the bus took over an hour to get to the stop. It would have been easier to get someone to take him, but the solitude that only this method provided was worth it to him. His thoughts were making circles around Ondrea, his mother, and Rick when the green neon lights, spelling out "Irruption Comics," appeared. The moment the bus driver opened the door, Sean leaped out as if he had committed a crime. He ran to the front of the store and stopped to get a good look at it. Irruption Comics looked like a small mom-and-pop store from the outside. The sign even had some lights on the letters that were either broken or had gone out. But walking through the door was like stepping into another dimension. It was incredibly bright and noisy inside. It was also deceitfully massive. Sean felt overwhelmed by all the different sections. It was like a Walmart dedicated to comic books and memorabilia. The store was packed with kids of all ages. Sean felt silly asking for help, plus he wasn't completely sure who worked there, so he continued to wander around. He saw a stand for the Inhumans, the Justice League, Black Panther, and Catwoman. *I wonder if Ondrea knows about this place.* Sean stood there at the stand gathering details to tell Ondrea, when some kids running around unsupervised bumped into him, and, out of the corner of his eye, he saw him.

As if it summoned him, the Paladin section was there waiting just for him. There wasn't another living soul around it or even near it. The section seemed to be in mint condition, untouched and untainted. There were shirts, mugs, pencils, and blankets with the "P" emblem. None of that really enticed Sean though. It was what was protected by the glass and lock that he desired. Sean stood there with his mouth open, staring at the last issue of the Paladin series. His pupils enlarged as he stepped towards the transparent cage that held the Paladin edition captive from him. The trance that held him was suddenly interrupted by an eerie feeling. Sean felt like he was being watched, but when he turned around no one was there. The area was completely desolate and devoid, which was odd since the rest of the place was so busy. Sean didn't notice the camera aimed right at the Paladin section and now at him as well, not at first anyway. When he did finally realize the surveillance, he shrugged it off and went back to imagining what adventures lived within those pages of the last Paladin.

Some time had passed when the strange feeling arose inside Sean again. This time, though, there was someone physically behind him. Sean turned around to see a slender man of Asian descent, not very tall, wearing a light blue collared shirt. The man wasn't smiling. At first, he stared at Sean, studying him. Sean's instincts told him to run, so he stepped back to get some distance before he took off, but the display corner was now against him. When the man finally did smile, the sight still made Sean uneasy.

"Hello," the man spoke in a monotone voice.

Sean didn't respond.

"I see that you are interested in the prestigious Paladin comics."

Sean nodded slowly, realizing the man worked there.

"Do you have any questions about Paladin?"

Sean didn't like the man, or he didn't like the feeling the man gave him, but he forced himself to speak, or rather mumble the words, "Yes, sir. May I look at the last issue behind the glass?"

The man pulled on a set of small keys that were attached to a stretchable string that was latched onto his belt loop. The man took a step forward to the case, and Sean moved out of the way like he was dodging a bullet. The man narrowed his eyes on Sean while sliding one of the keys into the slot, not diverting his glare for a second.

The man forced himself to smile again. "Here you go?"

Sean's excitement was swiftly deflated as he opened the comic and found only cardboard.

"Well, you did not think I would give you the actual comic to hold, did you? There is only one copy in the world. It is priceless."

Sean shook what felt like a fog out of his head. "Why is there only one copy?"

"Rumor has it that the creator Bao Eldritch was on his deathbed when he finished this masterpiece. It was his dying wish not to have it published." The man sounded like a robot.

Sean gazed at the front cover to absorb every detail of the image. Paladin on his knees with a look of anguish across his face. A man that Sean did not recognize from the other editions, laughing maniacally in the background. He took in the complete duende of the graphic into his soul. "Why didn't he want it published?"

"It has been said that there was a family dispute over the last issue."

"Hey, Alec. Your break is over. Back to your register," a round short woman with a clipboard called out from down the aisle.

"I am aware of that, Peggy." Alec took the fraudulent comic from Sean and placed it back behind the glass.

"Why do you have a fake one locked up?"

"Having the mock comic locked up gives the impression of having the real one to customers." He pulled on the string again to lock the case. "Have a good day," he said as if reading a script before he walked down the aisle. As he turned the corner without looking back, his words about the creator and his last wish rang in Sean's head.

*****

When Sean got home, everyone was hugging Loretta.

"Hey kiddo, your mom got a job at the library," Larry announced.

"You're going back to work?" Sean asked.

"Yes, Honey. Only part-time for now. I start tomorrow."

"This will be good for her," Bernadette affirmed.

Sean knew his grandmother was right. He remembered using the library back home to research projects for school. It would be a nice place for his mother to start, he imagined. At that moment, a light bulb went on inside his head. "Can I come with you tomorrow?"

"If you like, sure. I'll be working for four hours, but it's actually not too far from here so you can go home whenever you like."

"Can I come too, mommy?" Vivi pulled on Loretta's pants.

Loretta scooped her up in her arms. "Not this time, Love. But I'll make a deal with you. I'll check out five books to read to you this week."

"Six books."

Loretta pretended to mull it over before agreeing. "Deal." She leaned in and gently rubbed her nose against Vivi's.

Chapter 25

Sean felt foolish, not realizing before the obvious idea of looking up the author to learn more. At the library, he used the most modern means available to gain knowledge about Paladin's creator. Sean spent most of his time there researching at an available computer.

The first image he discovered showed a young, half-Asian man with his hair slicked back. The picture was dated 1963. The caption read, "Eldritch 26 years old makes his comic book debut." It was a magazine article that interviewed the upcoming star. The article was short, only a paragraph that summarized the hero Paladin. The details were nothing new to Sean. The next photo said 1970, but this time the man had silver sunglasses on and was in a wheelchair. *Did he get hurt or was he sick?* The article attached didn't mention anything about his health, only that Bao was receiving the Goethe Award. The rest of the article was about the comic book award itself. The only other information he found was of Bao in a newspaper from 1974. The heading read, "Paladin's Creator Found Dead". Sean was shocked by the photo. He quickly did the math in his head. Not once, not twice, but three times. Bao was only thirty-seven if the year was correct, but he looked like he was in his sixties. The piece had a bio about Bao's life. He was abandoned by his parents and left at a foster home when he was only five years old. He had a difficult childhood. Bao was the only boy at the foster home who was Japanese. There was another picture in the article. It showed a group of boys in front of a building named St. Selina's Home for Boys. The caption stated that it was unknown whether Bao was actually in the photo since the files at the foster home had been damaged after being exposed to mildew.

Sean learned how Bao's only outlet at the home was his stories. He was unable to answer how he came up with Paladin or his epic battles. Bao told an interviewer once that he thought they were told to him by a very old man from his early childhood, perhaps a relative of some sort before he was given up. Eventually, Bao was reunited with his family through the published comics. They were able to locate him again through Paladin. Sean wondered if seeing the people who gave him away was a happy reunion. Thoughts were racing through his head, but he was snapped back to reality by the sound of his mother's voice. She was speaking to a man.

Sean rose from his chair and followed the voices to the young adult section. He stopped one aisle from where his mother stood and peeked through the spaces created from the different heights of literature on the shelves. The smell of the old books made him nauseous. Sean could see his mother, but the man she was conversing with had his back to him.

"Thank you for showing me around, Mr. Barnes." Loretta placed a book on the shelf from her cart.

"Please, call me Harvey. If we're going to have dinner tomorrow, we should be on a first-name basis at least, don't ya think."

Sean jumped back like he was possessed. He felt a pain in his stomach as he charged over to confront them. He saw a short man out of shape with a balding spot smiling at his mother.

Loretta laughed softly. "You're probably right."

Sean felt the spin of the earth.

"Oh, hey Sean. How's the research coming along? This is my son, Sean. Sean, this is Harvey."

Harvey put out his hand. "Nice to meet you."

Sean ignored the gesture, and with wounded eyes, he glared at his mother.

Loretta saw his pain. "Harvey, can you please excuse us?"

"Of course."

Loretta stepped towards Sean, as he stepped back from her.

"Sean, please?" Loretta pleaded, trying to get close to him.

He turned his head towards the exit. Loretta knew it was futile to try to stop him, instead, she just breathed out the words, "I'm sorry."

Sean heard her say it, but he couldn't tell if it was for him or for Harvey. He didn't turn back to find out. He didn't care. He was happy to obey the voice inside his head. So, he ran.

Chapter 26

Sean ran past his house, not ready to go home yet. Past the school he would be attending in less than six weeks. Past a field where men were playing baseball. He heard the familiar sound of the bat hitting the ball. He heard voices cheering, then yelling, but he wasn't sure if they were real or memories. He began to see Rick coming at full speed towards him. Sean thought he was having that dream again. The dream was different this time. This time Rick was running towards him, not Ondrea. Sean stopped his legs at that moment. He looked around and realized the men were yelling at him. He wasn't dreaming. Sean looked up to see that a baseball was coming right at him. A second later, a hand was on his chest. The hand covered his entire sternum completely. Another hand was in front of him holding the ball up.

Sean lost his footing trying to step back, but Rick caught him also. Ondrea came running over.

"Sean are you okay?"

"Let's get him home." Rick helped him balance.

"No, I don't wanna go home," he managed to say.

Rick turned back to Ondrea. "Can you guys go back to your house? I think he's just dehydrated."

"No," Ondrea responded forcefully. "My room is a mess right now." She spoke quickly as though she had the excuse waiting and ready.

Sean's eyes were suddenly distracted by the reflection of Rick's belt buckle. He realized in that moment that it had a "P" instead of an "R."

"Just for a glass of water, Dre."

"No," she repeated herself. She looked around the field for an excuse. "It's getting late anyway."

Rick glanced up to see that the sun was still in the middle of the sky, but he read her cue to let it go. "Alright, I can take you both to the store…"

"Your house is closer. It'll be easier to get him water there," Ondrea suggested.

Rick was reluctant, but he agreed when he didn't hear Sean protest. "Fine, my truck is over there."

"Does everyone own a truck around here?" Sean mumbled.

"Pretty much." Loretta winked with her dark eye.

One of the players came over to check on Sean. "Is the kid alright, Rick?"

"He's fine Steve. Just needs some water. Let me know who wins, okay?"

"You know we're ahead by eight, right?" Steve chuckled.

"True. Alright, see ya at work tomorrow then."

"See ya." Steve ran back.

Sean let Ondrea lead him to the truck as he played out every moment and memory of Rick. His body was on autopilot as he climbed in after Ondrea. They drove six blocks to Rick's house.

"Wow, Sean. You're lucky Rick was there and that he's so quick. Another second and I think we would be making a different kind of trip." Ondrea leaned over to Rick. "Does your hand hurt?"

Rick looked over his left hand while keeping his right on the wheel. "Not really."

"I always forget you're left-handed."

Sean remembered the dinner from two nights ago. *Was Rick eating with his left hand*? Yes, because when Sean grabbed his plate, Rick placed the fork down with his left hand.

Ondrea shook her head and paused for a second. "You're like a superhero."

Rick chuckled softly. The words echoed in Sean's head. They got out of the truck and Rick told them to stay on the porch while he got everyone a bottle to drink.

Sean sat on the top step. "P."

"What?"

"P."

"You have to go."

Sean shook his head, "Why a P on his belt?"

"Oh," Ondrea giggled. "P for Patrick."

Rick came out and swung the screen door closed. He carried all three bottles in his left hand. He handed them out, then leaned against a column by his front steps.

"Why don't you go by Patrick?" Sean asked, holding the bottle of water with both hands.

Rick shrugged. "People started calling me Rick when I moved here, and it just stuck."

"How long ago was that?"

"Um, about fifteen years ago, I guess. I don't really keep track."

"Where were you before? Where were you born? Why did you leave there?"

"You're very talkative today. Are you okay?" Ondrea put the back of her right hand against Sean's forehead to check his temperature.

Sean didn't let her soft touch deter him. "What state exactly?"

Rick took a big gulp from his bottle and then placed the cap back on. "Alaska, believe it or not."

"Really? I never knew that. How come I didn't know that?"

"Don't know, Dre. You never asked."

"Or you never shared. I can't picture you in Alaska."

"Alaska was my first home. Well, first home I remember. It's where the hospital was. You know, where I woke up." Rick finished the bottle.

"The coma." Sean stared into the distance as he put the bottle down next to him.

"That's right. Now drink." He gently nudged the bottle closer to Sean with his Timberland.

Sean opened it and began to drink slowly.

A few minutes went by where Sean couldn't comprehend what they were saying. They served only as noise in the background of his thoughts.

Uncle Leo said he was real. Am I crazy? Could Rick be...

"Come on, Sean. Walk me home." She pulled Sean off the steps. "Thanks for the water, Rick. Oh, and for saving Sean's life."

Rick waved from the top step of his porch. Then stood with his arms folded across his chest.

"Paladin's stance," Sean uttered under his breath.

"What?"

Sean turned back and forth between her and Rick, who was going back inside his house. He contemplated telling her his new revelation but quickly dismissed the idea. He needed evidence first.

Chapter 27

Ondrea wouldn't let Sean walk her all the way home. He knew why so he didn't push. When he got home himself, he ran straight into his room and locked the door. He made a beeline to his Paladin collection. Ondrea was right. Paladin was left-handed, but Sean knew that wouldn't be enough. And he knew if he mentioned the stance, he would be laughed at. His eyes surveyed an image of Paladin about to battle Alios. His pupils enlarged as they came across Verendus. *That would be the proof needed,* he told himself. The first comic, just titled *Paladin*, had given some background information on the iconic weapon. It was made of Damascus steel by a skilled blacksmith during medieval times. It was buried under Earth's soil in a protective case until the chosen one came for it. Paladin had it at every one of his battles. It was in every issue. Sean knew what he had to do. Find Verendus. His plotting was interrupted by a gentle knock at the door. Sean figured it was his mother and chose to ignore it.

"I know you're in there," Nana B's voice called out.

Sean got off the bed to let her in and returned to his spot. She closed the door behind her, walked over, and sat on the bed next to him.

Bernadette dove right in. "I know it's hard for you."

Sean quickly stared at his exit.

Bernadette got back up and opened the door. Sean gaped at her in bewilderment.

"If you don't like what I have to say you can go for a run." She walked back over to the bed. "But I would like a chance to be heard first."

Sean let his muscles relax and Bernadette knew she had the green light to continue as she sat back on the bed.

"We have not spoken about your father, since we lost him. I did not make you talk about it that day, the day you moved in, and I am not going to make you talk about it today." She paused for a moment to gather the right words. "But your mother. She has been hurting too, you know. She has hurt more than you know and more than you have."

Sean's eyes showed his disbelief.

"It's true because she feels her pain and yours." She swallowed hard. "And it's time for her to start letting go of that pain and continue with her life."

Sean glared at her accusingly.

"Now, she is never going to forget about your father or even try to replace him." She paused again for a second. "Ever. Those shoes are too big to fill, but she deserves to be happy again."

Sean looked away from her, still angered by her words.

"I don't know if this is too adult for you to understand, but I hope you will at least try because your mother will always put you and your sister first even if it means making herself miserable."

Bernadette stood up and leaned over to kiss Sean's head. "No matter how you handle this, I appreciate you hearing me out." She walked over to the door. "Open or closed?"

Sean knew what she was truly asking. He shrugged and picked up a comic book.

"You got it." She closed the door.

Sean chose to focus on other matters for the time being. He was going to make it his mission to find out more about Rick. To find the proof. To find the truth. To find Verendus. Tomorrow he would start his mission.

Chapter 28

Sean set his alarm for six in the morning just to be safe. He brushed his teeth, washed his face, and threw on some clothes. Sean didn't expect anyone to be up at that time. He was startled when he saw Larry sitting down drinking coffee at the kitchen table.

"Hey, morning kiddo." Larry closed the newspaper he was reading. "What are ya doing up so early?"

"Couldn't sleep," Sean responded quickly.

"Wanna go fishing? It's early enough to get some fine trout."

Sean blew out his cheeks. "Actually, I was going to look around the neighborhood to... familiarize myself more with it. Just needed some fuel to get me going." He grabbed a sesame seed bagel and began munching on it.

Larry chuckled. "Well, haven't you done that already with all that running around and all?"

Sean pretended his mouth was full to stall. "Yeah, but I was running. So, everything was a blur. I'm going to walk around this time instead." *Not my best work*, Sean thought to himself as he took another bite out of his bagel.

"Alright, maybe another time then."

Sean finished chewing. "Definitely. See ya later."

"Bye, kiddo." Larry picked up his paper with a disappointed look on his face.

Sean made his way to his destination and leaned against the side of a fence that was directly across the street from Rick's. Out of sight to do some recon. He vowed that he would stay there all day until there was an opportunity. Sean was still munching on his bagel when Rick came out with a tool belt in his right hand and keys in his left. Sean watched as Rick opened the car door and got in. He couldn't believe his luck. He told himself, *the universe is on my side.*

Sean pushed his back against the fence completely until he couldn't hear the truck anymore. When the coast was clear he walked the perimeter looking around periodically to ensure that no one would see him. The moment he felt it was safe, he was up like a monkey on the sycamore tree that he had knocked into the other day. The climb up might have looked flawless to anyone watching, the landing was anything but. He fell and scraped his elbow on the inside part of the fence, Sean noticed a bit of blood but wiped it on his basketball shorts. Once he was on his feet, he made his way over to a gray shed. He didn't make any attempt to open it when he saw the bolt lock attached. Sean figured he might find a key or something in the house. He hoped he would anyway. He moved cautiously to the sliding back door, doubting it would be open. To his surprise, it was. *Thank you, universe.* The place was dark. The sun wasn't up yet to assist him in his illegal search, but he managed to find his way to a lamp. The room was unimpressive. There was a lazy boy chair in the middle, similar to the one Larry had, and in front of it was a medium-sized television. On the stand next to the chair was an empty beer bottle from the night before, or even that morning. To the right was a fireplace, with a stack of firewood nearby. "He loves his firewood," Sean said out loud to himself.

To the left was a bookshelf that reached almost to the ceiling and took almost the whole wall up. It was filled from top to bottom. Sean recognized some of the names from his mother's collection *Hamlet, Candide*, and *The Crucible*. Some other titles he couldn't figure out. He pulled one book out. It said, *Clizia*. Sean pursed his lips in disbelief. It was hard to imagine Rick as the scholarly type. He pondered if Paladin was. Sean remembered some of Paladin's quotes sounding intelligent. But was that Paladin or was that Bao? Sean couldn't remember exactly where he'd pulled the book from, so he guessed its place and went on his way.

Sean climbed the stairs and found the bedroom to be the next on his list to search. It was painted the same rustic red color as the living room. Sean didn't want to rifle through Rick's underwear or anything like that, so he limited his rummaging to only the nightstand drawers and the closet. He opened the bottom drawer first, nothing but more books. Then he opened the top. There was one book with a photo being used as a bookmark. Sean leaned against the twin-size bed and studied the picture. It was Rick sitting up in a hospital bed smiling with a nurse standing next to him smiling as well. He looked almost exactly the same, except in the photo his beard was unkempt. Sean squinted hard to see if any details should jump out to him. He flipped the picture over and read the back. *"Patrick and Kalon 1971"*. Sean looked up staring at the wall contorting his face. *How could this be that old? It looks like it was taken yesterday. This picture is*…. He paused calculating the numbers in his head. *It's 20 years old.* Suddenly, Sean felt his head spinning. He laid down on the bed and closed his eyes. When he was able to, he opened them and noticed a mural on the ceiling. It looked like an ocean. He laid there for another minute studying the details of the waves in the painting. *Rick stares at this every night. This means something.* Sean couldn't figure it out, so he placed the photo back in the book on page 51 just where he found it. He read the title, *One Hundred Years of Solitude*, and then placed the book back the way it was discovered.

Sean straightened out the bed, then checked the closet. He was still hoping to find Verendus. Nothing but clothes and more books. Sean made his way to the kitchen and inspected every drawer, shelf, and appliance looking for any kind of key. He felt silly checking the fridge and microwave, but he had to rule out any hiding places. It wasn't until he closed Rick's refrigerator door, that he felt vindicated. Two pictures of Rick. One with him next to the nurse and a boy not much older than Sean. The other was with the same individuals after an obvious time frame. Rick looked exactly alike, but the woman and teen looked substantially different. The woman's hair was no longer jet black, but halfway gray in the top picture. She also had more wrinkles and lost some weight in her round face. The teen was now a man who had grown over a foot taller from his adolescent years. Sean took both down from their Alaskan state magnets to analyze them better. He turned them over. One said "1972," one year later from the picture in the bedroom. The other said "1983." Eleven years apart. This was proof.

Suddenly, Sean was startled by the phone ringing. The caller ID read Xavier's. Sean quickly put the pictures back on the frig with their magnets. The ringing finally subsided, and Sean felt less flustered. He took a deep breath but jumped again when he heard a man's voice.

"Hey Rick, it's Barry. Can you come in an hour early tomorrow? Let me know. I'll try again to catch you later if anything."

Does Rick have two jobs? Sean was suddenly struck with a brilliant idea. He went over and checked the answering machine. There were only two messages saved. The caller ID read Kalon Neige. *The same last name as Rick.* She sounded gentle and calm, but older in her voice.

"Patrick, it's me. I wanted to check in on you. Call me back when you can."

"Hey, Patrick. Just checking in. Call when you can."

After the messages ended, Sean glanced up at the clock that was hanging on the wall adjacent to the doorway. He had been there for over an hour and the sun was completely out now. Sean checked every room once more to ensure that there was no trace of him left behind. When he felt positive there wasn't, he went back to the backyard and closed the sliding door as smoothly as possible. He held his head high, feeling somewhat satisfied with what he had found. That feeling didn't last long when he realized he had no way of getting out.

Sean could not make his way back to the branch he fell from. The height was too great for him to reach. He considered stacking the firewood, but that would give away the fact that someone had been there. He had to risk climbing the shed that was in no way near the tree or anything else. He'd have to jump from the shed onto the outside ground. Sean knew this would hurt, but he could not see another way. He reluctantly climbed up, hesitated for a few seconds, and when he finally mustered the courage to go and possibly break both ankles, he heard, "Hey, felon." Sean almost lost his footing but regained his balance quickly to see Ondrea looking up at him.

"What's up?" She placed her hands on her hips.

"Okay, I know you probably have some questions."

"More than some." She put her eyebrows up.

"And I will answer them all, but first… can you please help me down?" Sean pleaded.

"Okay, give me a minute." Ondrea left Sean standing on the shed.

That minute was too long. Sean began slipping and fell to the ground. Luckily, the only thing that got hurt was his Yankee T-shirt. The right side ripped when it got caught on the corner of the shed. Sean picked himself up and inspected the newly made hole in the logo at the bottom of his shirt. Out of the blue, a yellow flying object landed next to him. It was a Frisbee. He looked all around but only heard the wind. For a second he thought Ondrea had abandoned him. That is until he heard the sliding door open. Sean froze like a deer in headlights as he could only make out a large figure standing in the doorway. The sun's rays made it hard to distinguish any other features. Sean knew there was nothing more he could do then but accept his fate. He was able to breathe again once he saw Ondrea standing next to the man in the doorway.

"Sorry again, Rick. It was my fault. I threw the Frisbee too hard."Ondrea stepped outside and put her eyebrows up again signaling to Sean to follow her lead.

Rick came out next. "It's okay, Dre. Next time though, tell Mrs. Quinn across the street. She has a key to the house, so this guy doesn't have to get hurt again." Rick pointed to the cut on Sean's elbow.

Sean looked down at his arm. He hadn't noticed that he was still bleeding. Rick picked out a small key among the others on his chain to unlock the shed. He then opened one door and entered. Sean leaned over to get a better look, but all he could see were tools. Rick closed and locked the shed while holding a toolbox.

"You wanna clean yourself up inside?" Rick gestured with his chin.

"You wanna come over for dinner tonight?"

Rick was surprised, but not as much as Ondrea.

"Uh, if it's okay with your family."

"It is," Sean quickly responded.

"Okay, then."

"Great." Sean gave Ondrea a look that said, "Let's go." Then he raced through the house.

Ondrea smiled at Rick awkwardly before doing the same.

"Hey, don't cha want your..." Rick picked up the Frisbee, but they were already gone.

Sean started lightly jogging so that Ondrea could catch up.

"Hey, Rick believed me. You didn't have to..."

"I wanted to invite him."

"So... You guys are cool now?" Ondrea queried.

"Very cool."

Ondrea grabbed Sean's arm and looked back at the house to make sure it was safe to speak. "Why? I mean, I'm glad. Rick's nice, but ya know, all of a sudden?"

"Do you wanna come over for dinner also?"

"Sure, but..."

"Let me go and tell my grandma and mom about it. I'll catch up with you later."

Ondrea looked at him puzzled.

"What?"

"Your eyes."

"What? What is it?" He started rubbing his eyes.

"They just look different."

"Good different or..."

"Good different," she stated.

Sean gave her a smile. "Okay, I should go. I'll see you later." He darted down the street before she could say another word.

Chapter 29

Sean convinced his mother to reschedule her date for another night. He had a plan, and it involved his mother being present.

In the early afternoon, Sean went around the neighborhood looking for Ondrea. He couldn't just go to her house, so he continued roaming until he saw two girls walking while giggling. They were both dressed in leggings. One wore a Marilyn Monroe shirt while the other had a shirt on that read, "I Know You're Jealous."

Sean suspected that these would be the kind of girls that Ondrea would never associate with, so he decided not to engage. Unfortunately, the girls had different plans.

"Hey, you're the new kid right?" Marilyn asked. "The one that just moved in?"

Before he could respond, Jealous sneered, "You're the one always with Onweirdrea."

Sean knew girls like this back home. He was even friends with some, in his other life. He didn't want to give them any kind of satisfaction, so he strolled right past them.

"Hey, ever wonder why you're her only friend," Marilyn called out after him.

"He's probably a freak too who's missing a toe or something." Jealous nudged her friend to keep moving.

"Too bad. He's kinda cute."

Sean felt a deeper connection to Ondrea now. A feeling of a stronger need to protect her.

He began running to Virginia Comics. There she was coming out of the store. She smiled and Sean couldn't understand why anyone would ever say a mean word about Ondrea.

"So, ya gonna tell me what's going on?"

Sean explained the plan to her, all except the why. *Not yet. I can't. I need more proof.* He promised her it would all make sense soon. Ondrea reluctantly agreed to the terms.

*****

That night Sean helped with dinner. His mother assumed it was to make up for pressuring her to cancel her date, but Nana B knew there was something deeper going on. She had her own theory and felt, if true, it would have a good outcome, so she did not press the issue.

When Rick showed up, it was Sean who greeted him the warmest.

"You forgot this at my house." Rick handed him the Frisbee.

Sean politely thanked him and, when no one was looking, flung it across the room out of sight. He helped Rick take off his jacket and was extremely insistent on him handing over his keys so that Vivi wouldn't have a chance to lose them. After hanging the keys up on one of the hooks by the front door, he sat him down in the living room and ran to the kitchen.

"I'm going to get Ondrea."

"Oh, what a gentleman." Nana B winked.

"Speaking of. We have a gentleman waiting in the other room. Perhaps, someone can keep him entertained until Ondrea and I get back. Mom?" Sean asked coyly.

"But..."

"Go ahead, Honey. I got it from here." Nana B untied Loretta's apron and pulled it off of her.

"Are you sure, mom?"

"Yes, she's sure." Sean pushed his mother through the kitchen door.

"Okay, I'm going. I'm going. You're acting very strange," Loretta whispered before heading over to Rick.

"Sean," Nana B called back.

Sean turned around to his grandmother.

"Good choice." Nana B stirred the chicken stew.

"You have no idea," Sean murmured.

"What was that?"

"Nothing, Nana. Got to go."

Sean proceeded to sneak past the living room without being spotted by Rick or his mother. He grabbed Rick's keys by the end to ensure they wouldn't make a sound. He turned to check one more time that no one was watching.

"Shen, what are ya doing?" Vivi was rubbing her eyes from waking up from a nap.

"Nothing. I'm going to get Ondrea. You wanna play dolls with her right?" Sean spoke quickly and quietly.

"Yes, but..." She gave a very long yawn. "After I have my chocolate milk."

"Okay," he said in a hushed tone. "You go get it." He kissed her on the forehead before he gently pushed her forward. After she was out of sight, he silently slipped out the screen door.

Chapter 30

Sean met Ondrea in front of the park where Rick had saved his face from that baseball. She was waiting on a bench, reading a comic about Wonder Woman. She looked frustrated as her two different-colored eyes met his.

"Hey, you ready?"

"Not really."

Sean glanced down at his watch. "Why not?"

"You want us to break into his house." She paused. "Again."

"You never broke in. He let you in. It was just me last time and it will just be me this time, too. I need you to just be the lookout, remember?"

Ondrea bit her lip while shaking her head. "You're not even telling me the whole story here."

He grabbed her arm. She winced, but Sean was too focused on his plan to notice. "I promise when I can I will."

He stared between her brown eye and her hazel one. A calmness fell over him that he couldn't explain. He felt lost and found at the same time. Sean shook himself free from the trance. "We're good right?"

"I guess." She released herself from his grip. "For now."

*****

They hustled over to Rick's house as quickly and quietly as possible. Ondrea, unfortunately, did not remember which key would open the front door. Luckily, there weren't too many on the key chain. The fourth one was the charm.

Ondrea took her post while Sean made a beeline to the backyard, almost knocking down a lamp in the dark. The screen door was locked this time. He undid the latch and stepped outside. The streetlight was enough for him to see the keys and the lock. There was only one small key that would fit so Sean knew it was the right one. After opening the shed, he immediately found a string leading to a light and turned it on. Not too much to look at. Tools, lawnmower, mostly handyman stuff. He maneuvered around everything, careful not to move one item out of place.

Suddenly, the alarm on Sean's watch began beeping. He had set it for thirty minutes from the time he left. He couldn't believe that in all that time he didn't find the bow staff or any other proof of Paladin.

Sean locked up the shed, closed the back-yard door, and locked the house. Disheartened, he walked over to Ondrea. She took one look at him and decided not to push the matter. They walked to the house in silence. Sean's thoughts were foggy, but then he remembered the photos on Rick's fridge. Sean knew the truth. He knew it in his heart. And, he knew there must be other ways to prove it. He turned to Ondrea and said, "I made you a promise. I'm going to keep it. Tomorrow, okay?"

Ondrea agreed, "Tomorrow."

In better spirits, they began jogging back to his house.

*****

Dinner went smoothly. Sean was outgoing, social, and happy. It reminded Loretta of old times. Initially making her sad, but then grateful. She looked around the room, saw smiles, heard laughter, smelled chocolate cake, and felt family. Her eyes met Rick's after Vivi had given him an unexpected hug. Loretta blushed and looked away. Sean witnessed the interaction and thought if it must be someone. He decided to seize the moment.

"Rick wanna go fishing tomorrow with Larry, Ondrea, and me?"

Rick wiped his mouth with his napkin. "Well, I have to work tomorrow night, but I am free in the morning."

Bernadette elbowed Larry in the arm. "How come this is the first I'm hearing about this?"

"It's the first I'm hearing about it, too, Bernie," he pleaded with her not to hit him again.

Rick chuckled, "If Larry is up to it, sure."

Ondrea walked over to Sean and whispered in his ear, "You said tomorrow you would tell me what's going on."

"I know. I will. During our fishing trip," Sean reassured her.

Soon after, Rick drove Ondrea home, and it was once again quiet. Larry was asleep on the lazy boy, with Vivi asleep on his chest.

"I should take her upstairs." Loretta began walking toward them, but Bernadette stopped her.

"Let them sleep. I'll check on them after the *Tonight Show*."

Loretta agreed. She kissed Vivi and Sean goodnight before heading upstairs for bed.

"I'm really happy you invited Larry out with you guys tomorrow. I know it means a lot to him," Bernadette said to Sean.

Sean just shrugged it off.

"I know it's just another day for you, Sweetheart, but Larry misses that bonding between fellas."

Sean turned his attention away from the television to see his grandmother's intense dark brown eyes staring back at him.

"Ever since Clark…" She looked lovingly at Larry. "Well, he's been trying to fill that hole ever since. Right or wrong, that's what he's been doing for years."

"Who's Clark?"

"Larry's son. He joined the army when he was only eighteen. Larry was so proud. He bragged about it all over town." Bernadette laughed lightly. "He was on his third deployment when... Well, I don't know the whole story. I'm not even sure Larry does." Her eyes began to water.

Sean felt uncomfortable. Bernadette must have sensed it because she dropped the subject and said, "You should head to bed. You got an early morning ahead of you if you're going to catch anything."

"Goodnight Nana B." He kissed her on the cheek.

At the sudden display of affection, Bernadette responded, "Goodnight, my Sean Sean." A nickname only she called him.

Chapter 31

The next morning, Sean was up with Larry, loading the truck with fishing gear. Rick would meet them there and pick up the bait, while Larry and Sean got Ondrea. She was waiting at the corner of the street with a dismal look upon her face. She had a huge gray sweatshirt on that went down to her knees, with black leggings underneath.

"Ya know I don't believe I've ever met her father."

"I'm sure that's for the best," Sean breathed.

"Why do you say that?" Larry asked.

"Uh, no reason. Just ya know. He doesn't look very friendly."

Larry nodded slowly. "You're right about that."

Ondrea's bleak demeanor quickly changed as she climbed into the car. Whatever was on her mind stayed on that corner and was left behind as they drove away.

On the way to the lake, Sean paid special attention to the bridge they had to cross to get to the fishing arena. The wheels in his head were turning.

The fishing expedition was pretty uneventful if you were to only count the number of fish as your basis. Everyone had a pretty good time talking and laughing though, so to them it was not a day lost.

At some point, Sean had gotten up and gone over to the truck. He was glad to see that no one noticed. On the drive home, Sean's second plan went into action. The truck started to drive a little funny and soon enough it had a flat. Larry had no choice, but to pull over on the bridge.

"I guess I drove over some glass or something. I checked the tires this morning before we left," Larry said as Rick approached from his vehicle that was now parked behind them.

"No problem. I have a spare in the back." Rick started walking back to his car and Sean jumped out to walk with him.

"Hey, do you ever wonder about your life before the coma?"

Rick, stunned by the question, stopped in his tracks. "Excuse me."

"Like, who you were before?"

"Of course." Rick started to make his way to the back of his truck again.

"Well, I think I can help you with that."

"Is that so?" Rick chuckled.

"Yeah, I think I know who you were," Sean asserted.

"Do you now?" Rick picked up the spare and put it down on the pavement.

Ondrea was now out of the truck as well and was looking at Sean suspiciously.

"Yes, you are Paladin."

"Who?" Rick was carrying the tire back with one hand.

"Paladin, the great hero of Earth."

Ondrea's confusion was only outmatched by Rick's.

"Sorry kid, I don't know who that is."

"What's that now," Larry asked, holding his tire rod.

"Sean must be joking. Paladin is just a comic book character," Ondrea huffed, perturbed by the realization of the truth.

"It's true!" Sean defended his theory, looking solely at her.

"It's ridiculous!" She opened the back door of the truck and slammed it shut behind her.

Sean looked betrayed. He turned back to the men. "I'm telling you I can prove it." He watched as neither Larry nor Rick paid him any mind.

"Okay, I'll prove it then," he mumbled to himself. *Time for plan B.*

Sean began crossing to the other side of the bridge. Horns could be heard beeping at him, but it wasn't until he had already climbed over the railing that anyone took notice.

Ondrea's tightly closed mouth fell suddenly wide open as she saw him. She screamed before she opened the door. Both Larry and Rick looked in the wrong direction. Her door flew open, and Sean could hear her screaming for Rick to help. Without hesitation, Rick sprang into action. In a flash, he was across the bridge barely missing a semi-truck.

"What are you doing, kid?" Rick's voice started off calm.

"Just need to prove something."

"Prove something?" Rick looked down, shaking his head, then back up to Sean. "Look, I need you to climb back over right now."

"It's okay. I'll be fine. You'll save me before anything happens."

"You're pretty confident in my abilities, huh?"

"I'm going to jump, and you'll save me." Sean let his left hand go.

"This isn't a comic book, kid!" Rick thundered.

Sean looked down and stared at the river at the bottom. He knew he was right, but he was still filled with fear by the "what ifs?".

Rick composed himself. "Listen, I'm not really sure what's going on here, but I can't go back to your mother with you..." He struggled to find the right words.

Ondrea was now next to Rick, her eyes glassy. Larry had some trouble getting up and making his way over.

Sean took a deep breath and Rick lunged forward. "Wait, wait. Just wait a minute, please," he begged.

"Oh, God!" Ondrea called out.

Sean and Rick diverted their attention to her, then to what she was staring at.

Larry was doubled over in the middle of the road with his hand on his chest. Sean was frozen. He didn't notice Rick grabbing him and tossing him next to Ondrea.

"Stay!" Rick demanded with a voice of steel. He dashed to Larry and threw him over his shoulder.

Chapter 32

The ride to the hospital was quick. Rick drove recklessly. Larry had passed out from the pain. Men in uniforms put him on a stretcher and wheeled him in. Ondrea, without a word, without a look, without a thought, began walking home. Her house was at least four miles away, but Sean knew better than to try to convince her otherwise. Rick was standing by the automatic doors. The lights around the hospital covered his face with a shadow but Sean could still feel his daggers as he stood there in the parking lot. The silence was deafening. Rick turned around, giving Sean a chance to run. And he ran, he ran until he puked. Then he ran some more.

It was over an hour later when he made his way back to the hospital. He was positive his mother would put him away in some mental facility after what he had caused.

Loretta and Bernadette were both in the waiting room by then. Sean saw Rick leaning against the wall. His head was down, and his hands were in his pockets. Loretta had been holding her mother's hand when she jumped up to embrace Sean. Bernadette was in no state to stand at that moment.

"Honey, I'm so glad you came back. I know this is hard, but we need to stay together."

"I'm sorry."

"Sorry for what?" She kissed his forehead.

"I'm sorry for..."

Rick cut him off. "It's not your fault, kid. It coulda happened anywhere."

"But it was..."

"Your idea to go fishing. People have lots of ideas," Rick said, emphasizing the last word.

Sean realized he was giving him another out. He took it as any twelve-year-old would.

"Rick's right. Fishing didn't cause this. Come sit down." Bernadette beckoned Sean.

He sat next to her. She glanced up for a moment with a forced half-smile. In that moment, Sean could see how hard she was trying to hold it together. A sight he was not used to seeing. Her eyes went back to the white and black tiled floor.

Then a slender doctor in blue scrubs came out. He looked like he hadn't shaved or slept in days. "Rumson."

Bernadette cleared her throat and waved her hand. "Here."

She and Larry had never married. Sean never wondered why until that moment. It was obvious that they would be together for the rest of their lives, even with the kicks under the table, and elbow jabs everywhere else.

Dr. Batson told the family that Larry was fine but that he wanted to keep him in the hospital for a few days to run some more tests since he had a mild heart attack.

Bernadette put her hands to her mouth in relief while Loretta hugged her. Other than standing up straight, Rick hadn't moved a muscle until Bernadette reached her hand out to him.

"Thank you, Rick. If you hadn't gotten him here so fast–I don't even wanna think what would've happened." Her voice was shaky.

"He would've been fine because he knows he has you to come home to."

Bernadette laughed, and one tear escaped out of her right eye. She hugged Rick. Loretta watched and when her eyes met his, she once again looked away blushing.

Rick said his goodbyes after making everyone promise to let Larry know that he had waited for the good news. Sean stared as Rick walked through the automatic doors. He knew it was a bad idea, but he followed him to his truck anyway.

Rick put his key into the lock and said without turning around, "No need to thank me, kid."

"I just... I just wanted to show you," Sean stammered.

Rick sat in the driver's seat and started the ignition. "There's nothing to show." He slammed the door and drove off without any hesitation.

Chapter 33

It had been five long days since the incident. Larry was home recuperating. He didn't seem to remember anything about the bridge or even the flat tire. Sean was even more attentive to him than Bernadette. He continued his runs but made conscious decisions about which roads to avoid. Or rather which people. He didn't know if Ondrea would speak to him ever again. Loretta after rescheduling twice went on her date after all. Sean was powerless in any attempts to foil it. He had given up hope on trying. He decided to at least make amends with Rick since he, Paladin or not, was the hero who saved Larry.

Rick was sitting outside his house on the steps smoking a cigarette.

Sean was a little stunned by the sight. "I didn't know you smoked."

"Only when I'm stressed. I had quit a year ago." He rubbed the end on the floor before tossing it.

"I came to tell you that I'm sorry." Sean stared at the cigarette.

Rick took a slow deep breath. "Okay."

"Okay? Really? That's it?" Sean's eyes were full of surprise and doubt.

"Yeah, if you're man enough to come here and admit that you were wrong, then we're good."

Sean wasn't used to this. He'd become accustomed to a long speech about why he couldn't do whatever he was sorry for, how to improve on himself, and which chores he had to do to make up for it.

Rick stood up towering over Sean. "Now, what about Dre?"

Sean shook his head. "She's too angry. She won't forgive me."

"We don't apologize because we want forgiveness. Well, that's not why we should anyway."

Sean recognized the beginning of a lecture. "I know."

"We apologize because it's the right…" Rick looked away suddenly, and in the next second took off running without a word.

Sean watched perplexed, but in his peripheral vision, he saw black smoke.

There was no thinking, his legs followed Rick's.

Sean had gotten extremely fast with all his experience, but he didn't stand a chance in this race. He didn't see Rick go into the house when he finally caught up, but he knew. It was what Paladin would do.

Neighbors were beginning to crowd across the street. Sean swallowed hard and ran in after him. The fire was raging. The heat and smoke made Sean feel dizzy. Rick was carrying an old woman in his arms. She was unconscious.

"Get out of here, kid. I don't need a reason to come back in here."

Sean could hear the fire engines coming. He quickly turned around to leave when he saw a wooden beam give out. It happened so fast that Sean couldn't react except to shut his eyes and prepare for the pain. It didn't come, though. Sean opened his eyes to see Rick holding the beam up with his right hand while still holding the woman in the other. The flames danced around Rick's hand.

"Run!"

Sean looked around to see the house almost entirely engulfed in the blaze.

"Run!"

He heard the command again. Sean realized it wasn't the voice inside his head. Rick's eyes were hard and firm.

*****

Sean sat on the curb with a man checking his vitals. Across the way, a woman was doing the same to Rick. The old woman had been whisked away in an ambulance. There was an intensity in Rick's eyes. Sean couldn't distinguish if it was anger, disgust, or fear. All he knew was that it was aimed at him.

Suddenly he felt arms being thrown around him.

"You're crazy, you know that?" Ondrea said sobbing.

"I'm okay."

Ondrea pulled away. "I'm still mad at you."

"You're fine. Just drink this." The first responder handed him a bottle of water. Sean nodded and the man walked away.

"I know you are," Sean mumbled to Ondrea.

"I'm glad you're okay," she paused. "I'm glad Larry is too."

Sean opened his mouth to talk but no words came out.

"I'm going to check on Rick."

Sean watched their interaction. They both looked back at Sean several times. Then she made her way back over.

"How is he?" Sean asked genuinely.

"He's fine. Says he's just hungry."

"What about his hand?"

"What about his hand?" Ondrea repeated confused.

Sean jumped up and made a beeline. He grabbed Rick's hand, turning it over and back again. Then he grabbed his other hand and did the same.

"What is it, Sean?" Ondrea asked behind him.

Sean stared at Rick, who stared back. Finally, Rick gave the slightest head shake that was missed by Ondrea.

"Nothing." Sean swung around to her. "I just wanted to make sure Rick was okay," he lied.

Ondrea gave a suspicious look and tone. "I gotta head back before my dad gets home." She turned away and began slowly jogging.

"Can..." Sean stumbled over his words. "Can we hang out tomorrow?"

Ondrea stopped but didn't turn back. "I can't. I have family obligations."

Sean couldn't tell if she was lying as well, but he found himself relieved because he needed to focus on other things. He watched Ondrea until she was out of sight. When he turned back, Rick was standing directly in front of him.

"You know where the abandoned train track is?"

Sean had passed by the area multiple times during his daily runs. "By the old mill?"

"That's right. Meet me there tomorrow at 7 a.m.," Rick grunted as he walked away.

Chapter 34

ean was so hyped that he barely slept. He went for a quick run to settle his nerves and was at the railroad by six forty-five. Seven rolled by, seven fifteen and seven-thirty were much slower. The only other living thing there was a German shepherd behind the fence in some lot. By eight, it looked like Sean had been stood up. He was about to call it quits when he saw Rick's truck come into view. Rick got out and threw his cigarette to the side.

"I thought you might not come."

"You were right." Rick took off his sunglasses exposing his green eyes.

"Right about you being Paladin?" Sean asked hopefully.

"I meant about not showing up." Rick took a loud breath. "I know something is wrong with me, but I… I don't know what it is. I was thinking about it last night. I've never been sick that I can remember. Never gotten hurt. Hell, I've never even had a paper cut. I mean… Maybe this is part of the amnesia."

Sean shook his head forcefully and retrieved a comic from his backpack. It was issue four of Paladin, *The Return of Evil*. It showed Paladin in chains, while an evil-looking woman embraced him.

Rick's face contorted. "You gotta be kidding me." He grabbed the comic book, shook his head, and gave it back. "What am I even doing here?" he said, more to himself, turning his back on Sean.

"Why are you here? Why did you ask me to come?" Sean narrowed his eyes.

"I don't know." Rick threw his head back to the sky. "This is all just… crazy. I invited a ten-year-old to help me contemplate my life."

"Crazy but it all makes sense. And I'm twelve."

Rick ignored him and closed his eyes feeling the sun warm his face.

Sean moved to stand in front of him. "You know it makes sense. That's why you're here."

"I called Kalon last night."

Sean remembered the name vaguely. "Who?"

Rick opened his eyes and looked at Sean. "The woman that found me. That's her name. She was the nurse that brought me to the hospital." He paused as the memory flooded his senses. "She took me in and helped me get back on my feet. I lived with her and her son for thirteen years."

"Thirteen years?"

"They were the only family I knew." Rick tucked his lips in.

"What did she say?"

"I asked…," he trailed off, "I asked her to tell me about me." He paused and then exhaled hard. "I asked another person to tell me who I am."

"What did she say?"

"You're missing the point."

"What did she say?!" Sean demanded.

"She made a joke about finding a lost man." Rick turned away from Sean again. "She didn't give me any answers. Maybe she doesn't have any either."

"Look, you want answers. I can help with that."

Staring at the clouds, Rick said, "Yeah, how's that?"

"To get answers we need to investigate questions. We need to run some tests. Just like scientists do."

Rick looked down at him. "Tests?"

"Yes. Let's see what you can do." A smile edged across Sean's face.

*****

The first test entailed Rick running as fast as he could. Initially, it wasn't impressive. Sean soon realized Rick needed some motivation.

Rick's pace immediately sped up once he realized what was chasing him. He moved like fire, and easily climbed to safety out of the reach of the German shepherd.

"That was faster than Carl Lewis!"

"Awesome," Rick said sarcastically as he tried to slow his breathing down. "Now what do we do about him?"

The dog was still jumping up and barking at Rick. Sean, who was up on the garbage bin from where he'd let the dog free, decided to improvise. "The next test is strength and humanity. Put the dog away without hurting him."

Rick threw his head back in frustration.

The second test took a lot longer to complete. Rick was bitten multiple times; but didn't shed a drop of blood. Eventually, the dog seemed to like Rick. They even started playing together. Once the dog was back in captivity, it was time for the third test, or at least Sean tried his hardest to convince Rick it was time.

"No!" Rick shouted, shaking his head.

"What do you mean no?"

"I mean no!"

"How can we see if you can fly if you don't jump off a building?" Sean explained.

"I don't need to jump. I know I can't fly."

"Just jump and if you really can't fly then just do the superman landing."

"I'll get hurt."

"You don't get hurt."

Sean tried, but Rick wouldn't budge, especially after learning that Paladin never flew in the comics.

"Okay, maybe we're just getting hungry. Let's go get something to eat."

Rick unfolded his arms. "That's the first good idea I've heard you say today."

"'First good idea I heard you say today,'" Sean quietly mocked Rick as he followed behind him.

"I can hear you."

"Of course you can. Superhero hearing!" Sean ran to the passenger side, swung the door open, and jumped in.

*****

Rick took Sean to Kara's, the diner on the corner of Bay and Killian Road.

They were seated at the counter and were given lunch menus since it was now the afternoon. A waiter named Scott began taking Rick's order. Sean was perusing the menu when out of the corner of his eye he saw– "Mom?"

Loretta turned her head. "Sean?" She was just as surprised. Then she blushed when she noticed his company. Sean blushed when seeing hers, but for different reasons.

Harvey got up before Loretta did. "Hey Sean, it's really nice to see you again."

Sean nodded.

"So, you fellas are having lunch too?" Loretta asked.

"I'll come back." Scott flipped his notepad closed.

Sean searched for a normal answer when Rick took off his hat, ran his left mitten through his hair, and replied, "Sean was helping me clean my shed in exchange for a free lunch." Rick had his sunglasses on, which reflected Loretta's disbelief.

"Really?"

"Oh, that's a relief," Harvey said with a small chuckle.

Everyone turned to him with inquisitive brows.

"Well, it's kinda strange for a man to be hanging out with a child," he explained, pausing for agreement. "Right?" He emphasized the word.

Rick pursed his lips, but it was Loretta this time doing the rescuing. "Rick's our neighbor who comes over for dinner from time to time."

"Oh, that's good." Harvey was trying to hide his obvious intimidation.

"Are you guys ready?" Scott was back with his notepad.

"Okay, we'll let you boys get back to it." Loretta kissed Sean on the head. "I'll see you at home, I guess."

"Okay, Mom."

Harvey gave an awkward smile with a silent wave.

Sean didn't want to wait for food any longer, so he answered Scott's question quickly with, "Just give me the same as Rick."

A footlong meatball sandwich was soon in front of him, along with a tall glass of lemonade. Some time had passed. Both seemed uncomfortable with Loretta and Harvey only a few feet away. When his mother and her companion got up to pay the check and say goodbye, both parties noticed the tension ease once the bell on the door was quiet from their exit.

Rick put the last bit of his sandwich in his mouth and between chewing said, "You didn't tell me about him."

Sean was only halfway through his. He waited to swallow before answering, "Who, Harvey?"

Rick wiped his mouth with a napkin. "So, he's okay for your mom?" It was more of an accusation than a question.

Sean placed his sandwich down in order to be taken seriously. "I'm not sure he's okay for anybody's mom."

Rick chuckled before downing the rest of his lemonade.

"I'm okay with you." Sean picked his sandwich back up.

Rick turned his mouth to the side. "Now that you think I'm Paladin."

"You still don't believe? You were there. You saw what you did today, what you did yesterday with the fire."

"Shh." Rick looked around to ensure no one was within earshot.

"And I know there are countless other feats that you can't explain." He took a big bite of his sandwich.

Rick held the empty glass in his hand. "I know something's up. That doesn't mean I believe all of your... theory. I mean even you have to admit, it's hard to swallow."

Sean shrugged his shoulders, moved the food to one side of his mouth, and said, "Hey, by the way, that was pretty quick thinking."

"What was?" Rick grabbed the check and stood up to get his wallet.

"The story you told my mom. Ya know. About the shed."

"Well, I figured it was partly true." He took out a few bills and placed them on the table.

Sean stopped chewing and stared at Rick, or rather at his own reflection in Rick's glasses.

"It didn't make sense at first. Nothing was stolen. Then I figured it out after the day on the bridge, but from here on out, permission is needed."

"Wait, how did you know..."

"You're not as slick as you think you are." Rick ran his hand over his hair before putting his hat back on. "Permission is needed, Comprende?"

Realizing he needed to work on his spy game, he agreed, "Comprende."

Rick headed for the exit and Sean stuffed the rest of his sandwich into his mouth.

Chapter 35

Rick let Sean play with the radio stations on the ride home. "Brown-Eyed Girl" started blaring out of the speaker. "And you, my brown-eyed girl," Sean sang along.

"Surprised ya know this one."

Sean gave a look of offense.

"You don't have to get sensitive. It's just kids today. The only music I hear is rap or grunge."

"Kids today," Sean mimicked. "You sound like an old geezer."

Rick smiled. Sean smiled back. "My dad played this song all the time." His facial muscles slowly relaxed. "Whenever he came home from a long deployment, he would sing it to my mom." Sean stared out the window. He could feel the adrenaline entering his veins.

"What happened to him?"

Sean focused on his breathing, trying to bring it down. It worked. He felt safe to be open with Rick, or rather with Paladin. "He was in the Navy. He came home September 15th." Sean paused for a moment. It was hard to say more than a few words at a time. "He was at the bank and... there was a man." Sean tightened his fists.

"I'm sorry."

"I just thought he was safe when he was home, ya know." Sean's voice shook.

Rick didn't know what to say so he just laid his hand on the back of Sean's neck. Sean didn't understand why, but it helped. They let the music play for the rest of the ride.

Sean got out of the truck and closed the door. Through the open window, he asked, "Are we on again for tomorrow?"

"I have to work in the morning," Rick said, leaning over.

Sean looked deflated.

"What about Wednesday?"

Sean grinned. "Okay, Wednesday. Don't be late this time. We only have five weeks before I start school."

"I won't. See ya Wednesday." Rick pulled out and put his hand up as he drove off. Sean did the same.

*****

When Sean walked into the house, Loretta was playing the board game *Sorry!* with Vivi at the dining room table.

"Got room for one more?"

"Always." Loretta smiled.

"Yay, Shen's gonna play. Yay." Vivi jumped up.

After some time, Loretta shifted in her seat. "So... you've been helping Rick?"

Sean couldn't tell what her intentions were but decided to seize the opportunity. "Um... yeah. He needed help with his shed." He slowed his speech. "I... am... going... to... help... with... other... projects... too." He rolled the dice and moved his green piece nine spaces forward.

"My turn, Shen." Vivi grabbed the dice off the board and blew on them for good luck before tossing them. She moved four spaces up.

"Well... I... think... that's... a... good... idea." Loretta playfully imitated his tone while rubbing the dice.

"Me too. I think it might be a good idea for you to spend more time with him also." Sean gave an innocent look.

At hearing these words, the dice slipped out of Loretta's hand onto the floor.

"I'll get them, Mommy."

Sean's eyebrows shot up. "You okay, Mom?"

"Fine, I'm fine." She cleared her throat. "It's just that... I'm dating Harvey right now."

Vivi handed Loretta the dice again. Sean stared at his green piece, which was so close to being home.

"Sean, you're not mad at me, are you?"

"Mommy, roll the dice."

"Just a second, Honey."

Sean squinted his eyes. "No, I'm not mad. I understand." *I understand that this is going to take longer than expected, but I'm playing for the endgame*, Sean told himself.

Loretta smiled and gently threw the dice.

Chapter 36

The next three weeks flew by. Any morning Rick was off, he was with Sean testing his limits. He was fast, not Flash fast. He was strong, not Superman strong. He was durable, not Wolverine durable, but Rick was adamant about not being shot, so Sean wasn't completely sure. Every day Sean was with Rick, he tried his hardest to convince him that he was Paladin. He showed him similarities, commonalities, and parallels to the comics. Rick would just laugh it off and change the subject, usually to Loretta.

Sean had barely seen Ondrea since the fire. They passed each other on the street from time to time, but she always seemed to be too busy for him, coming up with one excuse or another. He wanted desperately for her to be part of it, but he told himself that if she couldn't see, or refused to see, then it was better this way, for now.

School was starting in two weeks. Sean felt the pressure and the need to press on.

"I think tonight we should try out your skills."

"Isn't that what we've been doing?" Rick started the ignition.

"No, I mean try to save someone from–" He moved both his hands in a grand gesture, "--something. Of course, it would be better if we had Verendus."

"What's that?"

"Your bo staff. I showed you like ten times, remember?"

Rick shook his head.

Sean whipped out issue 6 of Paladin, *Finding Bolide*, from his backpack and pointed to the front illustration. "Look, you're holding it on the cover."

Rick glanced at the image and nodded to appease Sean.

"You never fight without it but until you remember where it is you'll have to."

Rick remained silent as he turned onto the main street.

"Right now, you need some field experience."

"Field experience?"

"To prove your heroism."

"My heroism?" Rick shook his head in disbelief.

"Are you going to just repeat everything I say?"

"It's just... a lot."

"Well, what did you think the goal was?"

"I–I don't know. I didn't think I'd be going out in tights pretending to be some superhero." Rick's voice was firm and hard.

"But you are a superhero! And who said anything about tights?" Sean was getting frustrated.

"This whole thing is getting too crazy for me. I thought I wanted to know." He looked at Sean then back at the road. "But the more we do, the less I feel... like I know myself."

"You're Paladin!"

"Again with this." Rick pushed his tongue to the side of his mouth. "You know what. I think I need some space."

"Space? What are you talking about?"

Rick pursed his lips and shook his head. "I've been thinking about taking a vacation."

"A vacation? From what?"

"Oh, I don't know. From my two jobs, from Virginia, from all these tests, from…" Rick stopped himself before he said anything more.

"From what?"

Rick glanced at Sean.

"From what? What were you going to say?!" Sean demanded.

"Just let it go, kid."

Sean tightened his fists. "Pull over."

"What? No."

"Pull over!" Sean started unlocking his door.

"Whoa. Okay, okay." Rick pulled his truck to the side. Before they came to a full stop, Sean leaped out and sprinted down the street.

Rick watched him for a moment, then leaned his head back against his headrest and closed his eyes.

*****

Sean ran until he was tired. He skipped dinner and went straight to bed using the excuse that Rick had fed him a big lunch. Two days went by, and Sean was still upset, but he told himself that what he was doing was bigger than him and his feelings, so he went to Rick's house.

When he got there, Rick's truck was gone. Sean swore that he was supposed to be off. He sprinted home and pulled out the work number that Rick had given him in case of an emergency. The man who answered said Rick had taken a leave. Sean didn't have Rick's other work number because, as Rick had put it, "It's not the kind of place a kid should call." It didn't matter anyway. Sean felt it in his bones. Rick was gone. But to Sean, Paladin was gone.

Sean went back to his old habits, back to his fortress of solitude, back to being alone. Running, reading comic books, running, avoiding everyone, and running. Ondrea had seen him a few times out there. She could tell something was wrong. On more than one occasion it was she who tried to reach out now. Her voice was always drowned out by the voice in his head. She even tried to come to the house to see him, but Sean refused to leave his room.

Nana B would have taken more action, but she was busy attending to Larry's recovery. Loretta wasn't sure if she should intervene with the anniversary of Robert's death coming up so soon. She distanced herself from Harvey to make more time for Sean, but she barely saw him except for when he came home for meals.

The next two weeks were like living the same day every day to Sean, no difference from one to the other. It wasn't until he saw Vivi modeling her new kitten backpack that he realized school was starting the next day. He watched as Vivi tried to put Lilly inside the backpack despite their mother's protests. Still dim, the light inside Sean's eyes showed that no change was going to happen just because of a new school year. Indifference blanketed everything and everyone around him. School starting tomorrow or the world ending had the same effect on him.

Chapter 37

At school the next day, Sean felt like he was on autopilot. He went to all of his classes. He behaved so well that he was ignored by his math, English, P.E., and history teachers. The science teacher, Mrs. Morgan, had a different pedagogy.

Sean had the late lunch period, but he didn't mind. He chose to eat alone even though he noticed Ondrea sitting by herself as well. He had found a corner in the cafeteria where it would be hard to spot anyone, especially a quiet kid reading comic books while eating a ham and cheese sandwich. When the bell rang, Sean gathered his belongings, keeping the comic book in his hands to read on the way.

Students rushed into the science lab, knocking the comic out of Sean's hand. Mrs. Morgan picked it up for him in the doorway.

"Alright, alright. There's no need to run. I know you love science, but you bumped into another student. Also, I'm going to change your seats next week anyway so don't worry about sitting by your friends."

Only one student turned around and said, "Sorry, Mrs. Morgan."

"You didn't knock my comic book down," she replied as she gestured toward Sean.

The student looked at Sean. "Sorry."

"Thank you, Pietro."

Mrs. Morgan looked at the comic and read the title, "*Paladin, Hero No More*. I'm more of an Avengers girl myself." She smiled at Sean handing it back to him.

"Thank you."

"So, you must be one of the newbies."

Sean tucked in his lips and nodded.

"Don't worry," she leaned in and whispered. "I won't call on you in front of the class." She straightened up. "Not for the first week anyway." She gave him a wink.

Just then Ondrea approached.

"Welcome back, Ondrea. We have another comic book lover this year." Mrs. Morgan gestured to Sean.

"Cool," Ondrea mumbled, avoiding eye contact with Sean as she went in to sit down.

*****

After science was art class, and then dismissal. Sean ran home at the sound of the bell and went straight to his room. Loretta watched from the bottom of the staircase as the door swung closed. At that moment, she decided to take more drastic actions.

Chapter 38

Rick had been in Alaska for more than a week now. He hadn't told a soul where he was going or when he'd be back. He even had the water and electricity in his house turned off. Mrs. Quinn across the street was picking up his mail.

Kalon was surprised but ecstatic to see him. Rick was like another son to her, but she knew something was wrong. It took time, but she finally managed to get him to open up. Rick had expected her to laugh at the lunacy of it all. She didn't though. She didn't laugh or smile. She didn't even bat an eye. Kalon had a very earnest look on her face as she digested all the words he said. After a minute or so, she slowly rose from her love seat and walked over to the mantle where there were pictures displayed. She picked up a framed photograph of her son Remy with his wife and Kalon's granddaughter.

Rick was up now standing behind her, waiting for the usual pearls of wisdom she gave. Kalon handed him the picture. "That's Remy with Anna Marie."

"I know, I was at their wedding six years ago. Charlotte's getting big."

"Yes, and very outspoken as well." She handed him another photo in a frame. "Do you remember when this picture was taken?"

Rick saw himself and Remy laughing at the kitchen table. "Uh, ten years ago?"

"Sixteen years ago." Kalon put back the other photograph to let Rick focus more on the one in his hands.

"Remy had more hair back then."

She laughed as she made her way back to her chair. "Yes, that is very true. Remy looks much younger while you–you look like you could have taken the picture yesterday."

Rick looked up at the mirror above the mantle and analyzed his reflection.

"You have not aged a day, my son."

Rick moved his eyes over to study Kalon in the mirror. "You don't seem very surprised by this."

She took a slow deep breath. "I knew you were different. I knew the day we found you. Who could've survived in those icy waters for a day, a week, or, as I suspect now, much longer? We never found any sign of a boat." She whispered to herself, "Just a man in the water."

Rick placed the frame down gently.

"Patrick, sit next to me."

He knew it wasn't a suggestion.

She grabbed his hand and held it with both of hers. "I'm not sure who you were before that day, but I know who you are now."

"What if it's true?"

"If it's true then you know your past. It's you, not your past that determines your future. You have a choice, no matter what anybody tells you."

Rick kissed her hand and smiled at her.

Chapter 39

*I*t was over a week later when Rick began packing to go back to Virginia.

"Heading home?" Kalon was in the doorway.

"Not sure if it's home." He zipped up the bag and faced her. "But I...," he stammered. "I need to go back. I left some things unfinished."

"I want to show you something."

Rick followed her to the attic. Kalon pushed away boxes to get to a door. She pulled out a key from her pocket and placed it into the keyhole. She turned to him and explained, "I didn't want to show you this until you'd made up your own mind."

She pulled out the bo staff. Rick's eyes grew wide at the sight.

"When I was a little girl, my grandfather would tell me stories that his grandfather told him, of a protector of the people. Over the years, truths can be forgotten or are so... incredible that the mind determines them as myths, tall tales, or lies." She stepped toward him. "They retrieved this days later after you were found. I thought about showing it to you then but..."

Rick gently took the staff from her staring at the craftsmanship. "Why didn't you?"

"I was not sure it belonged to you at first." She turned her lips in for a moment. "Over the years though, it has become more and more clear that it is yours," she paused, "Paladin."

Upon hearing the name, his eyes looked up at her at once and he saw her crystal blue eyes staring back at him.

"I just wanted you to be the one who made the choice."

"That's why you kept this from me." His jaw tightened.

"Contentment is not the easiest goal to achieve in life. Who was I to take that away from you?"

"I don't think I can go back to the way things were before... now that I know."

Kalon put her hand on his while he gripped the staff. "You have given enough of yourself in that life, but you know I will support you no matter what you decide."

Rick's face softened. He kissed her on the forehead.

She looked up at him and knew it was pointless to ask him to stay. He had already made up his mind. "Alright," she said as she exhaled slowly. "I understand. I'll drive you to the airport then." She walked back down the stairs.

Rick paused there for a moment, clutching the staff tightly.

Chapter 40

*L*oretta had arranged for her brother and the rest of his family to come down to see them, but only Leo was available since the kids had just started school. Leo had always been an upstanding garbage man, so his boss was fine with giving him some time off. Bernadette was a bit disappointed because it had been years since all her grandkids had been in her home at once, but she still welcomed her son with a warm embrace.

The first thing the family did was go out to dinner. Vivi insisted on Cracker Barrel for their biscuits. Since Sean wasn't making any requests, they decided to appease the little one.

Leo sat by Sean. "How's school going?"

Sean shrugged his shoulders. "It's only been a week."

"Prison is what I called it when I was a kid. Right, ma?"

Bernadette chuckled. "Yes, and your school did resemble a prison in a lot of ways."

"You remember Sister Natalia." Loretta's eyes almost popped out.

"How can I forget? I still have the mark from her crane on my shin." He pulled his long leg up in the air and pointed to a scar about half an inch long. "Helping me walk straight my butt."

"Things were different back then." Bernadette grabbed Leo's wrist and squeezed.

"That doesn't sound like an apology. Does it, Loretta?"

Loretta pursed her lips and shook her head. "Nope, no sorry there."

"I've never heard Nana B say sorry," Vivi said while shaking her head.

"And you probably never will," Larry whispered to her.

Everyone laughed except Sean who was moving his macaroni and cheese around with a fork.

Leo leaned over to him. "Hey, I got a surprise for you."

Sean looked up at him.

"Tomorrow, you and I are going on a little adventure."

Sean did his best to smile but fell short.

Leo tousled his hair gently. "You'll see you're gonna love it." Then he threw a paper straw wrapper at Loretta. "So, you gonna let me have the guest room or what?"

Loretta threw it back. "The couch has your name all over it."

Dinner went on with the same banter, but Sean had tuned out.

Chapter 41

The next day Leo took Sean to a bagel shop. They both got egg, cheese, and bacon sandwiches on everything bagels.

"This isn't the surprise by the way," Leo remarked as he pulled out of the parking lot.

Sean felt the warmth of the bagel bag on his leg. His stomach rumbled at the aroma.

Leo dived in and unwrapped his sandwich with his teeth and right hand. He took a massive bite and pushed the food to one side. "Dig in. It's better when it's hot."

Sean unwrapped his sandwich and slowly began to munch on it.

For the rest of the ride, Leo tried his best to keep a conversation going until he realized Sean was asleep, with only half of his sandwich eaten.

When the car finally stopped and was turned off, he woke up. Leo put the sunshade up. "Just stick your sandwich in the bag. Come on." He excitedly hopped out of the car.

Sean wrapped the sandwich back up and stepped out. They were in front of a huge house. Most would say a mansion.

Leo held his hands up. "Well?"

Sean's eyebrows pulled down in confusion.

"Oh, I'm so excited I forgot to say it." He ran over to Sean. "This was the house of Bao Eldritch."

Sean's pupils grew twice their size. A smile spread across his face that matched Leo's.

"Right?"

Sean nodded. "Right."

"We're going on a private tour."

"How did you do this?"

"It was a pretty penny, but I wanted to do something big for you this weekend."

Sean knew what tomorrow would be. He could never forget the date even if he tried.

"I wanted to do something special, ya know," Leo explained as he put his hand on Sean's shoulder.

Just then a tall slender woman of Asian descent stepped out. "Mr. De Luca." She reached out her hand to shake his. "I'm so glad you were able to make the trip."

Leo's hand met hers to shake. "Maryland isn't too far from Virginia, but I just want to say thank you so much for taking the time for this."

After he released her hand, she folded her hands together in front of her black, buttoned-up shirt. "Oh, it's always a pleasure to meet a fan of my father's work. This must be Sean." She stepped over to shake his hand. "Your uncle has told me so much about you."

Sean was starstruck. Leo leaned over and put his hand back on Sean's shoulder. "He might be the biggest fan you ever meet."

"I'm Maeve Eldritch, Bao's daughter. I'll be the one giving you the tour today." Her smile seemed genuine, but to Sean, her eyes looked empty. They reminded Sean of a robot, like the Terminator movie that he watched with his father, despite his mother's objections.

"We're just both so happy to be here." Leo pulled Sean closer to him.

"Please, follow me."

Leo guided Sean as they followed behind noisy heels. Sean realized that she was not as tall as she appeared. They entered the home and Maeve directed Leo to sign a log at a desk in the front while Sean took in the atmosphere. Paladin memorabilia was everywhere. There was a staircase that had two openings that wrapped around to the second floor and at the center of the room was a life-size statue. The statue was not painted, and Paladin did not have a beard, but Sean still saw Rick.

"How much is the statue worth?" Leo's eyes were full of amazement. "If you don't mind me asking."

"Eighty-seven thousand," she said proudly as she walked over to it. "The artist, Farren, had never even heard of Paladin. He, to my knowledge, has still never opened any of my father's comics."

"How did he know how to carve him then?" Sean asked, not diverting his eyes from the statue.

Maeve stared as well, admiring. "My grandfather directed him. A total of 121 hours. Let me show you the rest of the house."

"Grandfather?" Sean queried, perplexed. "Wait. Bao's father is still alive? Is he here?"

Maeve, ignoring his question, led them up the stairs. Sean let his hand glide up the railing. There were seven rooms on the second floor. Six of the rooms had a grand poster of Paladin, more collectible items, and figurines. They were not given access to the seventh room.

Maeve completely walked past it as though it did not exist. Sean looked up at Leo, who shrugged his shoulders and motioned him to keep walking. Sean could feel it in his gut, that was where he would find answers.

In a downstairs room, they were able to get a glimpse of the true final issue of Paladin, held in a glass case in a room with heavy surveillance. Maeve explained that it was never taken out during tours. The sight of his Holy Grail fueled him with the courage to ask about the seventh room, to which Maeve simply replied, "It's not on the tour." Her lack of elaboration made Sean's imagination wonder wildly. He felt uncomfortable asking her about her father's childhood, upbringing, or failing health. But he had to ask the one question that was burning inside him. Sean took a deep breath, and as Maeve was describing the Paladin fan club to them, he blurted out, "Is Paladin real?"

Maeve stared at Sean and then at Leo. It only lasted a few seconds, but the question seemed to have rattled her. She regained her composure, straightening her dress shirt and clearing her throat. "There are myths and tall tales of Paladin's existence." Sean shook his head in defiance as she continued. "But even if those were true, they began more than a century ago. As I was saying..."

"But Superman ages slowly so does Wolverine, and others too," was Sean's claim.

She gave Leo a look that was somehow both polite and annoyed.

"I'm sorry, but it is getting quite late, and I have previous engagements. I'm sure you understand."

"Uncle Leo, you know others." Sean looked up at Leo pleading.

Not wanting to let his nephew down, he racked his brain. "Um, Black Widow, Wonder Woman, Mystique."

"Name some guys," Sean whispered.

"As I was saying..."

"Magneto," Leo interrupted.

Maeve put on a smile that was obviously forced, whether she intentionally wanted it to be known or not remained a mystery. "Here is the information about the fan club." She handed Leo a pamphlet. "You can look at your leisure." She led them towards the entrance door.

Leo looked at the front of the pamphlet and then turned it over. "Will do." Smiling shyly, he said, "We really do appreciate all of this."

"Of course. Have a safe ride home." She opened the door, signaling them to exit.

Leo steered Sean through it. Sean quickly turned around before Maeve could close the door. "Isn't it possible that maybe... that maybe Paladin is still out there? That maybe he just forgot who he is?" he exclaimed.

Maeve's body language was confident, but her voice told a different story. "How could Paladin forget who he is?"

"Maybe from some head injury or something," was Sean's quick rebuttal.

The door closed and Leo put his arm around Sean. "We need to get back anyway."

Sean allowed Leo to guide him back to the car. He looked deflated until Leo said, "She didn't correct you."

Sean's eyes showed his confusion when he looked up at him.

"When you said, 'Paladin forgot who he is,' she didn't correct you. She said, 'How could he forget?'" Leo pursed his lips and looked back at Sean, whose smile had grown from ear to ear.

*****

Maeve watched from behind the curtain as the car left the driveway. She walked straight upstairs to the seventh room. The room that was off-limits during the tour. She lifted her right hand to knock, but instead fixed her blouse first and then knocked.

"Grandfather, are you awake?" She hesitated before speaking again. "The boy that was here. I... I think we should discuss it."

A deep voice boomed from the other side of the door. "Come in."

Maeve opened the door, stepped through, and closed it behind her.

Chapter 42

When they arrived back at the house, Sean was in higher spirits. Leo put his keys up on the holder and prepared for an "incoming" as he heard fast little footsteps coming at him. He caught Vivi in midair as she jumped towards him. "Hey, you're getting so big, Vivi."

Vivi giggled. "Guess who's here?"

Leo moved her to his right hip to hold her with one arm. "Who?"

A man's voice could be heard from the kitchen, along with Loretta's. The voice was too familiar for Sean to doubt it, but he still had to see with his own eyes. He walked slowly to the kitchen. Leo followed him holding Vivi, whispering in her ear, "Who is it? Who is it?" as she continued to giggle at him.

Sean appeared in the doorway. Loretta and Rick were laughing with their backs to him. He could see that they were cutting potatoes together. Loretta turned around first, smiling effortlessly. Rick turned around, smiling as well. Sean did not return their greeting.

Loretta wiped her hands on her apron and said, "Hey, look who's back."

There was an awkward silence between them all. Not even Vivi or Leo made a sound.

"Kid, I'm really..." Before Rick could finish his sentence Sean rushed at him, hugging him as tightly as he could.

Leo's mouth dropped open, but Vivi was there to push it back up. Loretta's eyes began to water as her eyes met Rick's, but this time she didn't blush or look away.

Leo left soon after that so he could get back to Toni and the kids. Rick stayed for dinner and Sean felt almost whole again. The only one missing was Ondrea. He wanted to make things up to her, but until he knew how, he decided just to enjoy that Rick... Paladin was back.

Chapter 43

Sunday was a quiet day where the family stayed together and shared stories about Robert. Loretta was thrilled that Sean was there listening. Some moments were hard for Sean to hear, but Rick's presence somehow calmed him. Loretta noticed this and convinced herself that was why she wanted to keep Rick near.

The next three weeks were a blur. Rick was over three nights a week and it was obvious to even Larry that there was something more between Loretta and Rick. Sean decided not to push the Paladin thing, at least for now. Rick didn't bring it up either, afraid to rock the boat. Loretta was still seeing Harvey, but it was only a matter of time in Sean's opinion. Of course, it was only a matter of time. He had found the only other man on earth that was worthy of his mother and was content with that for the time being.

Sean was more alert during class. He was making some friends at school. During lunch every day, he would see Ondrea sitting by herself. Every day she would wear a big sweatshirt that covered the one leg that was bent as she sat. Every day she would read comic books while she ate her lunch. Every day Sean would hesitate while he held his lunch tray, lose his nerve, and sit with the boys from his P.E. class. Every day he missed her.

*****

Loretta's birthday was coming up. October 6th was this Saturday. Sean thought it was the perfect time to cement the connection between his mother and Rick. Harvey was out of town visiting family. *It's now or never*, Sean told himself.

"Hey mom, can Rick come over for dinner Saturday?"

"Sure, Honey," she answered as she pulled cold cuts from the fridge.

Sean punched the air in celebration as he started walking out of the kitchen.

"I won't be there though. I'm going out."

Sean snapped back around. "Wait, what? Why?" He came back over to her. "Harvey's out of town, isn't he?"

"Yes he is, but Melissa and Liz are coming down for my birthday. And they want to take me out for the night." Loretta smiled proudly. "You want a salami and cheese sandwich?"

"Uh, okay, sure." Sean's brain was going a mile a minute.

"Also, someone called for you before. Said their name was Marcus Gelid and wanted to talk to you about some Paladin fan club."

Sean's mind had already been gone, but now so was his body. Loretta turned around with a plate in her hands to see that she was talking to herself. "Bon Appetit," she whispered as she sat to eat.

Sean zoomed to Rick's house, who was just getting out of his truck.

"Hey, kid."

"This Saturday you need to take my mom out."

Rick slowed his step. "Did she say that?"

"No, but you have to."

Rick regained his pace and walked up the front steps.

"I'm serious. It's my mom's birthday and Harvey is out of town and..."

Rick turned back as he interrupted, "It's Loretta's birthday?"

"Yes, and her friends are taking her out but..."

Rick unlocked his door. "Then she already has plans. And that's that." He opened it just enough to only let himself through the doorway. "Look, I'm pretty tired from work and I still have a shift at Xavier's tonight."

"Xavier's?"

Rick breathed out slowly, but loudly. "That's my other job."

"That's a nightclub, right?"

"Yes. Wait. How do you know that?" Rick was more alert. "You know what. It doesn't matter. I'll talk to you tomorrow." He began closing the door.

Sean put his foot in the way. "I know you like my mom."

Rick stared at him through the small opening. "Yeah, so. She's a good woman."

"And I know she likes you too."

Rick opened the door wide. "Yeah, how do you know that?"

"She's my mom. I know her."

Rick shook his head. "Sorry kid, that's just not enough evidence for me." He started closing the door again.

Sean pushed the door open this time. "I know because she looks at you the same way she looked at my dad." It was obvious from Sean's face that it was hard for him to admit this out loud.

Rick stared at Sean for a moment. "Okay, you figure it out and I'll..." He hesitated for a second. "I'll do it."

Sean smiled. Rick gave a half-smile back and said, "But right now, kid, I'm tired." He closed the door completely. Sean stood there for a moment contemplating and planning. Then he raced home.

He strolled back into the kitchen where Loretta was cleaning the plate. "Mom, where's my sandwich?"

Loretta raised her eyebrows. "Seriously?"

"I'm sorry. I had to tell Rick it was your birthday Saturday."

"Tch. Sean, I can't believe you bothered him about that. Why did you do that?"

Sean shrugged his shoulders. "Rick was happy to know. He smiled when I told him." He pulled out a chair from the kitchen table and sat.

"He smiled?" Loretta began to slowly smile at the news, then composed herself.

"So, this Saturday where are ya guys going?"

Loretta pulled out the chair next to him and sat. "I'm not sure. They asked me where I wanted to go but, honestly I don't know the area that well yet."

"How about Xavier's?"

"Xavier's. I've never heard of it. It's a restaurant?"

"It's a nightclub."

"Oh well, that's... no then. I'm too old for that." Loretta got back up.

Sean pretended to be nonchalant. "It's where Rick works."

Loretta sat back down at hearing the gossip. "Really? That's his second job?"

Sean nodded. "Uh-huh."

It was obvious that she was pondering the concept of seeing Rick there. "I don't know. Don't cha think I might be too old for that?"

"What are ya talking about? You're not old. Besides, the club is for more mature women."

"Rick said that?"

"Not in so many words, but yeah."

Loretta began beaming softly. She caught herself before she fell too deeply into her own thoughts. "So do you still want that sandwich?"

"I'd love a sandwich."

Loretta rose from the chair and opened the refrigerator again. Sean smiled to himself, taking pride in his handy work.

Chapter 44

$\mathcal{S}$ean could hear loud boisterous voices in the living room. He walked down the stairs in stealth mode, apprehensive to enter the living room before seeing who it was. There were two slender women with their backs to him. He recognized them as Melissa and Liz, his mother's best friends. Each one was gushing over Vivi, who stood before them shining over the attention.

"She's becoming such a ham," Loretta called out from the kitchen.

"And where's Sean?" Liz asked.

Loretta came out of the kitchen holding a tray of crumb cake. "Oh, he should be around here somewhere."

Nana B was behind her, carrying small birthday dessert plates, with metal forks on top. "That was so nice of you ladies to bring Loretta her favorite cake and save me a trip to the store."

Everyone laughed lightly.

"It was really Liz who suggested bringing the cake," Melissa admitted.

"Yeah, but it was your plan to come up and see Loretta," Liz added.

"Please sit, ladies," Nana B insisted.

Both sat down on the couch with Vivi in the middle.

Nana B, who was cutting while serving the cake, asked, "So what's the plan for tonight?"

"The place we're going is called Xavier's, right Loretta?" Melissa passed her cake to Vivi.

"Xavier's? Isn't that where Rick works?" Nana B narrowed her sights on to her daughter.

Loretta, who was sitting in the end seat, avoided eye contact, and dug into her piece of cake with her fork.

"Bernie," Larry called from the backroom. "Are we out of clean towels?"

"Excuse me, ladies." Nana B left the room and patted Sean on the shoulder as she passed. "They won't bite, sweetie."

"Who's Rick?" Melissa had a playful look on her face.

"I thought you were going out with Harvey." Liz's expression matched Melissa's.

"Harvey and I are not exclusive. He's not even here for my birthday."

"And, my question," Melissa reminded her.

Loretta put her fork down. "Rick's just a friend of the family."

"Just a friend," Liz echoed. "What does this friend look like?"

"He's big and tall and has lots of muscles," Vivi answered with her mouth full.

"Oh yeah, that sounds like someone you'd just want to be friends with." Melissa winked.

Sean tried to escape without being ambushed like Viviana, but the creaking of the front door betrayed him. Both Melissa and Liz attacked Sean with hugs and kisses on his cheeks. He looked to his mother to be his savior, instead, she savagely smiled as she ate the rest of her cake.

Thirty minutes later, the three ladies were climbing into a white buggy. Sean and Bernadette, who held Vivi in her arms, were waving goodbye. "Baby Baby" by Amy Grant was blaring from the speakers, drowning out any voices.

As the lyrics screamed, Vivi put her hands over her ears. "That music is too loud, right Nana?"

"You're so very right, Sweetheart." Bernadette rubbed her nose gently to Vivi's

Sean waited until the car was out of sight to start making his way down the street, but not before getting a nod of approval from Nana B. When Rick opened the door, Sean almost didn't recognize him. His hair was slicked back, which gave it a darker tone, and his beard was nicely trimmed. He was wearing a blue suit, a classic white shirt, and a black tie.

"Wow."

"I clean up nice, right?" Rick pulled gently on his suit jacket.

"Not bad." Sean nodded. "So, were you able to find it?"

"Yeah, it has a little something extra too. Come here." Rick had Sean follow him to his truck where he took out a large rectangular-shaped object, covered in light brown paper. Rick uncovered it to reveal a beautiful image of a forest with the milky way galaxy in the background. There was a quotation at the top.

"'I know nothing with any certainty, but the sight of the stars makes me dream,' Vincent van Gogh," Sean read out loud.

"I know you said to get her something with stars and nature, but there was something about this quote that reminded me of your mother. Plus, I know she loves Van Gogh."

Sean's expression showed how impressed he was by the gift. "Good job."

Rick sat in his truck not starting the ignition. "So, I just show up there. Even though I took the night off." He gently wrapped the gift back up.

Sean saw the doubt spreading across Rick's face. "Listen, you remember what we talked about. Make her feel like she is the only woman in the room."

Rick nodded as he placed the picture next to him in the passenger's seat and started the truck up. "Taking dating tips from a middle schooler," he mumbled to himself. He closed the door, pulled out of the driveway, and waved to Sean.

Chapter 45

Rick walked up to Xavier's entrance door holding the gift in his left hand. There was a stocky man with dark olive skin standing outside.

"Rick!" He put his hand out to shake. "I thought you took the night off?"

"Hey. Yeah, I'm off duty. Can't ya tell?" Rick raised his arms midway and did a 360 to show off his suit.

"Oh yeah. Looking fresh, bro. Is that a gift for me? Aw, you shouldn't have."

"Sorry, Victor. This gift has someone else's name on it." Rick started walking in.

"Go get her, Killer." Victor chuckled to himself as a woman walked up, showing her license.

When Rick walked in, he was surrounded by roaring music, flickering lights, and oblivious people. He stepped into the other world unfazed by the sights and sounds of the club. Through the crowd, Rick spotted Loretta standing at the bar. She was laughing with a man that he didn't recognize. Losing his nerve, Rick went to the left, walking behind a door that read staff only.

"Ricky, Baby. What are ya doing here?" A petite woman with fiery red hair turned around to him.

"Hey, Yukio. Just wanted to check in and make sure there wasn't any trouble." He sat in the computer chair next to hers, placing the gift on the floor next to his feet.

"On your day off, dressed like that, carrying a gift." She motioned her head towards his feet. "Yeah right. So, who's the crazy lady?"

Rick looked at her, puzzled.

"She must be crazy if she stood you up. Hell, if I was ten years younger..."

"I'd be in trouble."

"Yes, you would be."

Rick glanced at the small video screens showing the different angles of the club. "So, you don't need me?"

"It's been a pretty quiet night so far, Love." Yukio knocked twice on the desk in front of her.

Rick didn't respond.

Yukio exhaled loudly, "Go out there, and forget about her."

Rick didn't budge.

Yukio pushed his chair with her leg. "Go! Have some fun," she commanded.

"Okay, okay. I can see where I'm not wanted." He got up from the chair and began walking towards the door when he heard a commotion coming from one of the screens.

"Looks like I spoke too soon."

Rick's eyes became hard.

"I can just call Victor or Martin."

"Hey, I got nothing else going on."

"You might mess up that pretty suit, though."

"Here." Rick slid his jacket off, folded it gently, and placed it on the chair by Yukio. "Watch this for me."

"Alright Baby, but after this, promise me you'll have some fun."

"Promise." Rick moved swiftly out of the room while folding his sleeves up. He climbed the stairs to the second floor while loosening his tie.

At the top of the stairs were two men arguing over a spilled drink. Rick pushed himself through the mob that had now formed around them and put himself between the two men. The darker-skinned man close to Rick's height and size told the shorter paler man to relax.

"It was an accident," the tall man said firmly.

"If you weren't staring at my wife so hard you wouldn't have spilled your drink on me," the shorter man replied aggressively.

"Oh, come on man. I got my own chick."

"Alright, alright. Settle down." Rick was trying the calm method first.

"She's not interested in you." The short man pushed the tall man forcing him to step back.

Standing nearby was a short curvy woman giving daggers to anyone who locked eyes with her.

The tall man pushed the short man back. "I don't even want that rat-looking piece of..."

Before the tall man could finish his sentence, a blow came crashing into his jaw. Rick grabbed the shorter man to restrain him, but the tall man popped him back in the nose in retaliation. Everyone's attention was now on the commotion upstairs, even Loretta had her eyes fixated on the second floor.

"That's enough!" Rick yelled at the tall man while the shorter man approached again. Rick used the shorter man's momentum to flip him on his back and put the tall man in a choke-hold before he could get another shot in. Then Victor and another stocky man appeared.

"We got it from here, Rick." Victor took the tall man away while the other bouncer took the short one. "Get back to your day off."

Rick nodded, dusting his clothes off. From his position, he could see Loretta watching him. "Make her feel like she's the only woman in the room," he whispered to himself. He looked over at the crowd still on the stairs, and after some quick thinking, he climbed over the banister. Rick whistled at the group below him to move. Without any hesitation, he jumped down the one flight, landing perfectly on his feet. Loretta was still directly in his eyesight. Walking straight to her he ignored all other advances made at him. Rick stood before her gazing into her eyes and asked, "Can I buy you a drink?"

The man she was conversing with did not even try to protest, he just swiveled around to the female on his other side.

Loretta, speechless, just nodded.

"What would you like?"

"Just a regular iced tea. I don't actually drink."

Rick smiled at her, his eyes creating a mental road map of her facial features. Without looking away, he called, "Two iced teas, Raven."

The bartender brought the drinks over. Loretta took a sip of hers and then realized that her friends had suddenly reappeared. "Oh, I'm being rude. Rick, these are my good friends, Liz and Melissa."

"Hello, it's nice to meet you." Liz shook his hand first.

"Nice to meet you too." Rick finally pulled his gaze from Loretta.

"We were just going to go back on the dance floor," Melissa said as she shook Rick's hand, giving a knowing look to Loretta. "Come on, Liz. We'll see you guys in a bit."

After Melissa and Liz made their departure, Rick wasted no time. Confidently he asked, "Loretta, would you like to go out to dinner with me?"

Without hesitation, she responded, "Yes. I would like that."

Their eyes were locked on one another until Rick said, "Wait right here. I forgot something." He dashed across the dance floor and flew into the security room, where Yukio was holding the gift for him to take from her.

"Thanks." Then he raced back to Loretta.

He handed her the gift. "Happy Birthday."

She gently unwrapped the frame. After reading the quote, she looked up at him. Her eyes shined like the stars in the picture as she said, "I love it."

For the next hour, Rick and Loretta talked. They discussed favorite movies, books they'd read, and stories of Sean and Vivi. The kids were a welcomed subject into the conversation. Rick enjoyed hearing about how Sean was when he was younger. Liz and Melissa soon joined them for the next two hours or so until the group decided to call it a night.

Rick offered to drive Loretta home, and there wasn't one objection.

The ride home was full of laughter, smiles, and romantic glances. Being the gentleman that he was, Rick opened the car door for Loretta when they reached the house and walked her up to the porch.

"So, I'll pick you up next Friday at seven for dinner?"

Loretta nodded. "Friday at seven. And tomorrow for Sunday dinner."

"Tomorrow for Sunday dinner," Rick repeated. He leaned in and kissed her on the cheek. Loretta closed her eyes as she felt his touch and reopened them to meet his gaze. They lingered there for a small moment in time, before they both came in for a kiss. At the same time, Sean had moved the curtain in the living room to check if his mother was back. He witnessed their first kiss. It was bittersweet for Sean.

Chapter 46

*L*oretta broke things off with Harvey as soon as he got back into town. Rick was over almost every night. The family seemed to be complete, well almost.

Marcus Gelid called five more times in the next two weeks, but Sean didn't see the point in joining a fan club at that moment when he had the real thing in his life. He had plans for Paladin that needed his undivided attention. But there was something still gnawing at him. Sean missed Ondrea.

Sean went over to Rick's house for some advice. He knocked on the door, but there was no answer. Sean felt he had reached a level with Rick that would allow him to walk in without permission, especially since the door was unlocked. For some reason, Sean's gut told him not to call out for Rick. He quietly walked up the staircase. He saw Rick standing in his bedroom with the door halfway open. He was holding something. Sean took a step forward to see what it was. He attempted to be stealth, but one creaking step gave him away. Sean cursed in his head. Rick turned around swiftly.

"Maybe super hearing isn't one of your specialties after all. You didn't even hear me come up the stairs," Sean remarked with a smirk on his face that quickly vanished after he realized what was in Rick's hands. Sean flew down the stairs, but he was still not fast enough to get through the door. Rick caught him before he escaped.

"Get off of me," he demanded, flailing his arms trying to get free.

"Okay, okay. Just calm down." Rick let go of him slowly. "Let me explain."

"How long have you had it?"

"Look, I was waiting for the right time to tell you."

"How long have you had it?!" Sean shouted.

"I got it when I went to visit my family in Alaska," Rick answered in a defeated tone.

Sean felt his head spinning. He kneeled on the floor so he wouldn't fall over. "For over a month, you've had Verendus." Sean put his hands on his head. "You've known. You've known that you're him." His breathing was erratic.

Rick stared out the window and swallowed hard. "It's not that simple, kid. Alright? Things aren't always black and white."

Sean used his hands to get back up. "I think it's very simple. You're a coward!" he barked.

Rick looked at him. "You don't understand."

"There's nothing to understand! You are nothing but a coward!" Sean yelled with venom in his voice.

"Look. Maybe that's not who I am anymore. Okay? Maybe that's not who I want to be." Rick matched Sean's intensity.

"You don't want to be a hero?"

"No, maybe I don't."

"How could you not..."

Yelling over Sean, Rick answered, "Maybe I just want to be normal! Have a wife, a family, a normal life!"

Sean was screaming now. "You can't have that!"

"Why the hell not?! Huh?! Why can't I?!" Rick thundered as he beat his chest.

Sean's arms were waving erratically. "Because you're not normal! You're Paladin! You are Paladin!" Tears were forming in his eyes. His breathing was quick and his heart was racing.

Rick calmed himself down. "Why is this such a big deal to you, kid?"

"You won't understand."

"Try me."

Almost in a whisper, Sean said, "Because if Paladin was there. Then maybe... maybe my dad would still..." The tears streamed down his face. "You... are... Paladin."

Rick tightened his jaw as he turned his back on Sean. "I'm sorry... but I don't know that life." He paused. "I'm not him, kid."

Sean stood there broken. He wiped the tears from his face and walked towards the door. Before leaving he hissed, "You don't deserve my mother. You don't deserve anyone."

Rick didn't turn around.

*****

Sean ran until the tears dried, then he ran some more. Ondrea appeared in his view. Sean felt compelled to go to her. He always felt compelled to go to her, but this time he didn't fight it.

"Ondrea!" Sean howled.

She stopped in place, hesitating for a moment before turning around. Sean was only a few feet from her now. His breathing was heavy, but not from the run. Ondrea stared at him. Her gaze made him feel dizzy again.

"I'm sorry," he pushed out of his mouth.

"Sean, I have to get home," Ondrea stated plainly.

He stepped closer to her. "Please, forgive me."

"Have you been crying?"

"No," he lied. "I just want you to forgive me."

Ondrea shook her head. "It's been months. And not even a word," her voice cracked. "I... I can't do this right now." She turned away from him and began walking home.

Sean rushed up to her, grabbing her arm as a reflex. "Wait," he begged.

She winced in pain. Sean let go immediately. Then without another thought, he quickly brought her wrist to him with his left hand and pulled her sleeve up with the other. The source of her pain was revealed. Across her flesh, stretching from her wrist to her inner elbow was a massive welt. She snatched her arm away, yanking her sleeve back down.

He looked into her different-colored eyes as tears fell from them. "Ondrea," he breathed out.

"Just leave me alone!" She wiped her eyes as she rushed to get away from him. Sean wanted desperately to be her hero, but he knew he couldn't do it alone. He didn't analyze the current situation any more than that, out of fear that he might talk himself out of it. Sean bolted back to Rick's. He burst through the door that was still left unlocked. Rick jumped up as a reflex.

"You were right, kid. I should've told you. I'm still just..." Rick scratched the top of his head.

"Ondrea's in trouble."

Rick switched gears. "What? What happened?"

"Her dad. He's been hurting her. I don't know for how long."

Rick left the room and marched into the kitchen.

"Where are you going?" Sean questioned.

"Getting my keys. We'll get there faster in my truck." Before Rick finished his sentence, they were both out the door.

Chapter 47

Rick pounded on Ondrea's front door. A few seconds later the door flew open, and her father was standing there fuming, "Who the hell? Rick. What do you want?"

"You've been putting your hands on Ondrea?" Rick commanded an answer.

"Get the hell out of here!" He went to close the door.

Rick grabbed it and forced it open, making Ondrea's father lose his footing.

"Is she here, Bill?"

"Get out of my house before I call the police!"

"Good. Call the police. Then we can show them what you've been doing to your daughter." Rick's eyes were as hard as stone.

"I said get out!" Bill swung his right arm, but Rick stepped out of the way to grab it. Then Rick pulled Bill by the arm forward and with his left hand pushed on the back of his head to slam it against the wall, just hard enough to daze him.

"Ondrea," Sean called in the doorway.

"Dre's leaving with us."

"Over my dead body." Bill picked up a nearby bat and charged at Rick.

Fluidly, Rick grabbed a jacket, sidestepped Bill once again as he swung, and wrapped it around Bill's throat, then tied him to the adjacent coat hook on the wall.

"Go get her," Rick ordered Sean.

"Ondrea!" Sean climbed three steps at once to get to the second floor. He knew where her room was, remembering its location from that one night. He found Ondrea sitting on her floor, leaning against her bed with her Walkman balancing on her knees. She had the headphones on. Sean could hear the music from where he stood, though he could not make out the exact song or lyrics. She looked up at him with tears in her eyes. This time she didn't try to hide them. He kneeled next to her and gently removed her headphones.

"You're leaving, Ondrea. Come on." Sean grabbed the Walkman and helped her up.

When they walked to the stairs, Rick could be heard on the phone talking to the police, while Bill was struggling to break free from the coat hook.

Ondrea started to draw herself back at the sight of her father, once again enraged.

"It's okay. I'll walk with you." Sean put out his hand for her.

Ondrea slowly slipped her hand into his. They walked down the stairs together.

Rick hung up the house phone and gave Ondrea a calming smile. "You ready, Dre?"

"Where are we going?"

"We'll figure it out," Sean said with a look of determination on his face.

Chapter 48

Bernadette insisted that Ondrea stay with them for as long as she needed. Vivi insisted that she stay in her room with her. And Loretta insisted that if Sean and Ondrea were alone in a room that the door always remained open.

Two nights later, after dinner, Sean was sitting outside on the porch with Ondrea, looking at the stars.

"I think that's the Gemini." Ondrea pointed to the right.

"Okay."

"And that one is the Libra," she said, pointing to the left.

"Sure."

Ondrea pulled her eyebrows down. "Ya know we have a test on this coming up?"

"I know but, I don't know any of this stuff except the big and little dippers." Sean squinted his eyes at the night sky. He paused for a moment before saying "Ondrea, I'm sorry."

Ondrea pulled her focus to Sean.

"I should've…" Sean lingered on the words.

"It's okay Sean," she placed her hand on his. "We're good."

"No, but… Not just the not talking to you part, but also your dad. I…I should've known. I should've said something sooner."

Ondrea squeezed his hand. "Hey, we're good," she reassured him, smiling.

Sean smiled back. "Oh yeah, I forgot to tell you. I got invited to a fan club meeting for Paladin."

"Really, how?"

"You remember that my uncle took me to Bao Eldritch's house?"

"Yeah, I'm still jealous about that." Ondrea gave him a side-eye.

"Well, the fan club president must have gotten my number from Bao's daughter. He called me yesterday. Actually, he's been calling me a lot and my mom forced me to talk to him so he would stop bugging her and anyone else who answered the phone."

"Why is he so interested in you though?"

"I guess my reputation precedes me." Sean leaned back with his hands behind his head and a grin covering his face.

"Ha, ha."

Sean shrugged his shoulders. "Guess he found out I went to Bao's house. He invited me to a fan club meeting on Friday after school. Would you wanna come with me?" Sean wasn't really interested in going, but he thought Ondrea might like to. After having gone to the police station to make a report, he felt like she needed something to distract her. Luckily, the ADA said they had enough evidence in her videotape testimony that she wouldn't have to testify in court and see her father again.

"You know I want to come with you."

Sean looked away, trying not to blush.

"How, though?"

He looked back at her. "How what?"

"How did Bao's daughter get your number?"

Sean grimaced. "Not sure. Maybe when we signed in my uncle put my number down instead of his. That or maybe it was in the newsletter." He smirked.

"Yeah, I'm sure." She pushed him gently.

Rick opened the screen door and stepped outside. "Hey Dre, Vivi is requesting your presence at some cat dress-up thing." There was a look of confusion on his face.

Ondrea got up. "Oh yeah, we're trying outfits on Lilly." She walked over to the screen door that Rick reopened for her. "Hopefully we don't get killed putting the tutu on her."

Rick and Sean both laughed.

"Tomorrow we should study together," Ondrea said to Sean before stepping into the house.

"Definitely. I need it."

"Just remember the door stays open in your room," Rick reminded Sean.

"I know, I know. My mom already said that."

Rick walked over and sat by Sean on the steps.

"Dre seems to be doing better."

"Just had to get her out of that house and away from him," Sean agreed.

There was a small moment of silence.

Feeling some tension in the air, Sean reacted, "So what's up?"

Rick took a deep breath and slowly exhaled. "I was thinking maybe we should start; you know..." He tilted his head to the left and paused. "Training again."

"Really?"

Rick nodded his head slowly.

"What changed your mind?"

He tucked his lips in for a few seconds. "Dre." He paused for a moment and continued, "I was just thinking maybe I could help some other people, too." He rocked his head back and forth. Maybe?"

Sean's pupils enlarged as he jumped to his feet.

Rick stopped Sean before he could speak. "Hold on now. Just some small things. And just in this area. Okay?"

"Okay, that works. We can start small."

"Look, kid, I'm not making any promises." Rick pointed at Sean

"Okay, I get it."

"Do you?"

"Yes," Sean confirmed without blinking.

"I'm not committing to anything." Rick was stern.

"Alright. I get it."

Rick got to his feet and patted Sean on his shoulder as he turned to go back into the house.

Chapter 49

Rick and Sean trained three times that week. These times included Verendus.

"It must be muscle memory," Rick responded after being unable to deny how fluid each movement was with the bo staff.

"You don't remember anything? Not Verendus, your powers, being Paladin?"

Rick shook his head. "No, not a thing." He paused for a moment. "Well, there is one thing."

"What?!" Sean could not hide his intrigue.

"I remember waves."

"Waves?"

"Yeah, you know. Waves in the ocean. Then only waking up in the hospital."

The image of the mural from Rick's bedroom flashed inside Sean's mind. He wanted desperately for something else to click in Rick's, or Paladin's brain. Sean was silent for a moment then suggested, "Maybe it'll come to you after some epic battle."

"Maybe?" Rick was unconvinced.

"I have to go. Can you drive me back now?"

"What's the rush?" Rick was still spinning Verendus around his hands.

"I have a fan..." Sean didn't know how Rick would respond to learning about the Paladin fan club, so he decided to omit that detail or rather substitute it. "I mean I have a party to go to with Ondrea."

Rick grinned, "Oh, so you have a date?"

Sean immediately began turning red. "I didn't say a date. I said a party."

"A party that you're taking Dre to."

"It's not like that." Sean turned around and started walking back to the truck.

Rick followed over to the driver's side. "Okay then." He hopped in and turned the ignition on, but before lifting his foot off the break he reminded Sean, "Just remember the doors stay open."

"Please stop talking," Sean muttered.

Rick drove as he chuckled to himself.

Chapter 50

As soon as Loretta put the jeep in park, both Ondrea and Sean jumped out from the backseat. They ran across the massive lawn and waited at the front door for Loretta to catch up. The house was a small one-story structure but the area around the home more than made up for it. There wasn't another house for more than half a mile. Sean studied his surroundings and noticed a flag that was waving in the wind outside the house. It was a red sun with rays stretching out. The movement of the wind made it look as if the rays were reaching out to him. Sean focused only on this until Ondrea commented on the beautiful sounds coming from the windchime that was hung outside. Little suns and moons made gentle music together as the air touched them softly. When Sean saw his mother standing by them, he took a step forward onto the brown welcome mat and rang the doorbell. A woman dressed as a maid opened the door and ushered them in. Loretta came into the house with Sean and Ondrea to ensure that she had thoroughly vetted the place, along with Marcus Gelid. She knew the person that she had spoken with on the phone was not a child. She had to make sure he wasn't a creep either.

"Welcome, welcome!" was shouted across the crowded living room.

There were kids around Sean and Ondrea's age blockading the area. A slender man of Asian descent meandered his way through the horde of pre-teens.

"I'm Marcus Gelid." He enthusiastically grabbed Loretta's hand to shake.

"Hello, I'm Loretta and this is my son."

"Sean!" Marcus interrupted.

"That's right." Loretta faked a smile to be polite.

"I've heard so much about you." Marcus put his hand out to shake.

Sean took his hand. "From who?"

"I was going to ask the same thing," Loretta said, with the same smile.

"Maeve," Marcus bellowed, without breaking eye contact with Sean.

Maeve appeared through the mob at once and gracefully made her way over.

"You must remember Bao's daughter."

Sean nodded.

"It's nice to see you again, Sean." She put out her hand to Loretta. "Hello, it's a pleasure to meet you. I'm Maeve Eldritch."

Loretta shook her hand. "Loretta, Sean's mother."

"I'm the guilty one here. I called Mr. Gelid."

"Marcus." He was adamant.

Maeve continued, "I called Marcus after meeting Sean to inform him that there may be some competition for the title of Paladin's biggest fan."

Marcus raised his eyebrows playfully.

Sean thought it was strange how close the two of them seemed. He got an eerie feeling from Maeve and couldn't understand how anyone could be on such friendly terms with her. *Something must be wrong with Marcus. Guilt by association.* His mother must have gotten the same feeling which was evident from her facial expression.

"Are you really Bao Eldritch's daughter." Ondrea was starstruck.

"I am." She shook Ondrea's hand. "And who may you be?"

"I'm Ondrea. Sean's friend. I'm a big fan of Paladin, too."

"Lovely. Can I offer any of you some refreshments?" Marcus gestured to a table with canned beverages, such as soda and iced tea.

"I'm not sure we'll be staying. I have work early in the morning." Loretta tried to hide her concern.

"But you must stay," Marcus insisted. "Maeve brought the last edition of Paladin for a reading. And, as a fan, you know the last time it was read was over two decades ago. I, myself, the fan club president, haven't even read it yet."

Sean's eyes dilated. He looked at his mother and no words were needed. She already knew. There was no way they could leave now.

*****

It was almost an hour later. Loretta was making small talk with some of the other bored parents at the site. Sean and Ondrea were debating which Paladin edition was the best with a short, husky boy wearing a Cavaliers baseball hat.

"How long have you been a member, Adrian?" Ondrea inquired.

"About two years now."

"And, you come here every Friday?"

"No, we usually have our meetings at Ororo elementary"

"Wonder why Marcus changed the place to his home."

Sean wondered as well.

"No idea. This is my first time meeting the president."

Sean wanted to know more but before he could even utter a word their conversation was interrupted by Marcus' whistling.

"Please everyone take a seat and we will begin our read of the last edition to the Paladin series."

Loretta sat in the back with Sean and Ondrea next to her. Maeve came over to inform them that there were two seats up front reserved for Loretta and Sean. Loretta insisted that Ondrea take her spot. Sean felt embarrassed receiving so much special treatment, but he followed Maeve to his assigned seat.

"Alright, let's begin." Marcus had a pair of black gloves on as he gently removed the comic book from its protective case. He held it in front of a group of adolescents, who practically drooled at the sight. With the protective cover off, it was revealed to this generation that the last issue was not colored. A detail that surprised Sean.

Marcus walked over to a wooden podium and placed the comic book upon it. Maeve came up and handed him a pair of forceps. With the softest, most gentle touch and the biggest grin, Marcus opened the edition. He began to read, "The sky was full of darkness, but it was not night. The only light that emitted was from the fire in Paladin's eyes..."

Every soul in the room hung on every word he said. It was poetry even to the ears of the ones who were not fans. Loretta saw why Sean had been so engrossed in this world. It was true that some of the credit had to be given to Marcus, who read the comic like he had read it a thousand times before, but with just as much energy and love as the first time. More than once he locked eyes with Sean, and every time Sean felt like he was reading the comic only to him.

The setting was after World War II. The grandson of Hirendan and son of Iniquan, Mortalan had emerged to finish what they had started. He had been raised for this one purpose. Sean lingered on the details of Mortalan's upbringing. He was told from the age of four that he only existed to avenge his father and grandfather. Brainwashed from that day on into thinking he must take from Paladin what was rightfully his.

"Mortalan," Sean whispered to himself trying to embed the name into his mind. When they reached the halfway point where Mortalan had set a trap for Paladin, Marcus closed the edition as carefully as he had opened it. "It's getting late, boys and girls, so I'll stop here. We can pick up next week for the ending."

Marcus' words were met with groans and grumbles. He smiled back at their unrest. "I love how enthusiastic you all are. It's only a week. Plus, this way you can debate theories with one another."

One girl with extremely thick glasses shouted out, "Come on, can't you finish now? I want to know if Paladin gets electrocuted."

Another girl behind her declared, "He doesn't get electrocuted, I heard he gets blown up by an atomic bomb."

To this statement, a very gangly boy responded, "An atomic bomb, really? You know you can't believe everything you hear."

Ondrea leaned over to Sean whispering, "I heard the bomb theory, too."

Sean shook his head and without thinking let the words slip out. "No, something happens that knocks him out. He ends up in the Pacific Ocean, but I don't know how."

"Why do you think it has to do with the Pacific ocean?" Ondrea inquired.

Realizing what he had divulged, he replied, "Uh, I'm just guessing."

"Well, that is astonishing." Marcus and his smile were standing in front of them. "Tell me, how did you come up with that specific guess?"

Maeve seemed to appear from Marcus' shadow. "Yes, how did you come up with that one on your own?" Her tone sounded more like an accusation.

"Wait, is that what really happens?" Ondrea asked.

"The element of water is involved, yes," Marcus quietly revealed.

"But you said you hadn't even read it," Ondrea innocently recalled.

"Yes, well," he said, giggling. "I just couldn't help myself." He looked back and forth between the two children. "Could you?"

Ondrea shook her head. "No..., I would have read it at least three times before this." She waved her hands around the room. "And, I know Sean probably would have read it twice as much as me." She nudged him.

"Yep." Sean cleared his throat. "At least that much." He wasn't sure whom he was trying to convince. Sean was more concerned with finding an escape from Maeve's murderous glare. He saw his mother waving at them and took the opening. "Well, my mom needs to get back home for my sister."

Ondrea turned around and Marcus looked up to see Loretta.

"Well, you'll be returning next week, correct?" Marcus asked eagerly.

"Of course. I have to know how it ends. As it is, I'll be losing sleep until then." Ondrea stood up next to Sean, who was already up and moving away.

"And you as well?" Maeve honed in on Sean.

This time Sean evaded eye contact. "I'll have to see." He was reluctant to turn his back on Maeve, so he tried his best to walk backward while steering clear of her scowl.

"You'll have to see? Are you joking?" Ondrea was appalled.

Sean, who almost tripped over another guest, grabbed onto Ondrea for support.

"Oh, I do hope you will. I always love when we get new members for the fan club," Marcus said warmly.

Both kids waved goodbye as they made their way through the maze of teens and pre-teens back to Loretta, who once again read Sean's body language. "I got your coats." She led the way out of the house. Sean turned around once before exiting to see that Maeve had yet to deter her stare. When they got outside, Sean shook off the bad juju and hustled toward their jeep.

Once inside the vehicle, Ondrea wasted no time. "So, what's going on?"

"I don't know. I just got a really bad feeling from her."

"Her? Who, Maeve?"

Loretta agreed with Sean's statement. "She's strange. I mean I don't want to be mean, but she seems off. I don't know. It's also a bit weird that a grown man is inviting children over to his house." She pulled out onto the main street.

"I think he's just a kid at heart. And Maeve, she's maybe a bit eccentric." Ondrea shrugged her shoulders and turned her hands over. "But aren't most kids who have famous parents?"

"Her parents weren't famous. Only her dad was," Sean reminded her.

"Excellent vocabulary." Loretta looked into the rearview mirror at them and then returned her eyes to the road.

Ondrea smiled shyly. Sean looked over at her, puzzled.

"It's one of our vocabulary words, Sean. Eccentric. For Mrs. Parker. Remember she said, 'the more you use the words the more you'll become familiar with them.'"

"I think that's an excellent habit," Loretta remarked.

"Sean, we still need to study the constellations. Our test is Monday."

"Tomorrow for sure," Sean promised.

"Okay, tomorrow." She fidgeted with her seatbelt. "So, we aren't going back next week then?"

Both Ondrea and Loretta looked at Sean for the final verdict.

Sean took a deep breath. "I guess it wouldn't hurt to go back just one more time to hear the end of the comic book. I mean Marcus does seem nice."

Ondrea tried her best to conceal her excitement but was unsuccessful.

Sean was still apprehensive about Maeve, but it made him content to see Ondrea so happy.

Chapter 51

The next day Sean and Ondrea spent the early afternoon studying. Breaks included snacks, comics, chasing Vivi, and brushing Lilly. During one of their many breaks, Sean overhead Larry talking to a man in a pickup truck out on the street. They were discussing how someone had been breaking into people's houses in a neighborhood about twenty minutes away.

"Larry," the man called as he brought his truck to a slow stop.

"Hey, Charles." Larry wiped his hands on a dirty rag and threw it on the car he was working on.

"Did ya hear about the break-ins down in Castle Gate?" Charles remained inside his vehicle.

Larry walked closer. "Yeah, I read it in the paper. They think it was someone who lives in the area."

Charles shook his head and grimaced. "What kinda world are we living in if we can't even trust our own neighbors?"

"I couldn't even tell ya." Larry spotted Sean on the porch. Deciding that the conversation was not age-appropriate he quickly ended it. "Alright Charles, I'll catch up with ya later. I gotta get back to this Pontiac."

Charles just gave a wave as a response while driving away.

Sean knew this was Rick's next opportunity. He felt as if fate was handing him a gift. Another chance for Paladin. Maybe Rick would even begin to remember who he was, who he needed to be. Sean told Ondrea that he was going for a quick run to burn off some energy, which was partly true because he ran all the way to Rick's place. When he arrived, he informed Rick of all the intel he had obtained from Larry's conversation.

"Alright. Tonight I work, but I can start doing recon in the area tomorrow night." He was making himself a sandwich.

"Okay, what time are you picking me up tomorrow?" Sean spoke casually.

Rick's demeanor quickly changed. "Okay kid, I know you are pretty invested in–" He searched for the right words. "--me. But if these are real criminals..." He opened a jar and inserted a knife.

Sean interrupted, "I was there when you rescued Ondrea."

"That was different." Rick slathered the bread with mayonnaise and then placed the knife in the sink.

"Ondrea's dad is a criminal." Sean was adamant.

Rick placed ham and cheese on the bread. "Yes, he is, but..."

"But what?"

Firmer now, Rick answered, "Look, I told you I wasn't making any promises." He closed the jar and placed it back in the fridge.

"Even heroes need helpers."

"You mean sidekicks?" Rick raised his eyebrows as he sat down.

"No, well... something like that."

"It's too dangerous, alright? And, anyway, not all heroes had helpers. You should know that. You're the comic expert." He squeezed the sandwich together.

"I never said I was an expert. And all the best superheroes have someone that assists them in some way."

Rick took a bite and with his mouth full responded, "You mean like Superman."

"Yeah well, you can't fly. And Superman joined the Justice League, where he did get help. Too much help, to be honest."

Rick swallowed. "Bottom line. I am not putting you in danger. Helper or not. Are we clear?"

Sean was quiet for a moment, not because he was offended or angry, but because he was planning. "Fine."

Rick was drinking from his glass of water but quickly stopped to narrow his eyes on his target. "Fine?"

"Yeah, it's fine. I understand."

Unconvinced, Rick placed his drink down. "Just like that?"

"Just like that."

Rick peered at him from the side. "All of a sudden you're fine with it."

Sean sat down at the table. "Yes. Are you going to keep asking? I'm fine with it because that's what heroes do. They protect others. You're thinking like a hero now so I'm fine with it."

Rick used his tongue to get a piece of food out from the side of his teeth. "Honestly kid, I didn't think you were going to be so mature about it. I figured you would end up running out of here yelling some insult at me or something."

Sean stood up. "I am going to run out of here, but only because I have to get back to studying."

Rick nodded. "With the doors open, right?"

Sean gave Rick a dirty look and then headed for the door.

"Hey, tell Dre I said hello." Rick heard the door close and smirked at his own joke.

Chapter 52

The next night Rick was in his truck watching a neighborhood in the Castle Gate area. He was eating a Twinkie while drinking a can of iced tea.

Twenty minutes later, Rick was fast asleep.

Sean, who was hiding in the backseat, threw off the blanket that was hiding him at the sound of Rick's snoring. "Hey, you call this recon?"

Rick woke up, startled. "It was just a power nap."

"Yeah right." Sean climbed into the front seat. "What do you expect when you eat junk like this?" He picked up the Twinkie wrapper.

Rick snatched the wrapper from him. "Now you're critiquing my diet."

"I'm just saying most people on a stakeout drink coffee and eat light." Sean folded his arms.

Shaking his head, Rick said, "What do you know about stakeouts? Wait! What are you even doing here?!"

"You're drinking iced tea."

Rick raised his voice. "Hey, I told you this was too dangerous."

"I'm not afraid," Sean affirmed.

"You're not afraid? Really?!"

"I'm not. And don't yell at me."

"I'm not yelling," Rick yelled.

Rick looked out the window, and then back at Sean. "Okay, maybe I am." He paused for a moment to calm down. "So you're not even a little scared?"

Sean shook his head. "Nope."

"Well, I am."

Sean looked at him in disbelief.

"Yeah, I am. I'm scared that something might..." Rick was interrupted by a loud noise.

"What was that?"

"Shh." Rick scanned the area.

A cat came running out of a backyard.

Rick relaxed but did not turn his attention away from the neighborhood. "I'm not even sure which street to be looking at."

"Well, this spot is good. It shows a connection to three streets."

"So glad you approve." Rick rubbed his eyes with the palms of his hands.

"You boys lost?" an unfamiliar voice asked.

Rick went to lower his hands.

"No, let's keep those hands up." An old man stepped out of the shadows with a gun in his right hand. A revolver that was not yet pointed at them.

Rick kept his hands high enough for the man to see them. "No, sir. We were just sitting here talking."

"You boys live around here?"

Sean and Rick answered the question simultaneously, but only Rick's answer was the truth.

"Well, which one is it?"

Rick glared at Sean.

"Ya know there've been some break-ins around here." The old man stepped closer.

"Yes, that's why we're here," Sean responded.

Rick moved his hand as a signal for Sean to stop talking.

"I said keep those hands up," the old man growled.

Rick put his hand back in place. "Sir, as you can see it's just me and the boy. Obviously, we're not the ones breaking into people's houses."

"Ain't nuttin' obvious except the fact you boys aren't supposed to be here."

"We're trying to catch the criminals," Sean clarified.

"Sean, stop talking," Rick said through his teeth.

"Is that so?" The man paused, then without turning his gaze he shouted, "Barbara, call the police."

"Sir, I'm going to step out of the truck so I can show you that I am unarmed and to show you my license so you can see that we are not criminals."

The old man stepped back in agreement. Rick slowly and cautiously got out of the truck. He gave Sean a stern look before closing the door.

"It's just you and the boy here?" The old man was trying to peer into the bed of the truck.

Rick, keeping his distance, answered, "Yes. This is all just a misunderstanding. I would like to show you my ID now so you'll know who I am."

The old man nodded. Rick pulled his wallet out of his front pocket and opened it. He held it up to show his license.

"Take it outta there."

Rick struggled for a moment to retrieve his license from the tight slot. Then he went to hand it to the old man, who was initially receptive in receiving the identification, but let the ID fall to the ground at the sound of a loud thud. The old man aimed his gun in the direction the sound came from, pulling the trigger before registering the image in his peripheral vision.

Ondrea was there in the cargo bed.

Sean should have known how much they thought alike. She stood there stunned. Sean was frozen as well, except for his eyes. He moved his eyes back and forth from Rick to Ondrea. He saw Rick grab the gun from the old man. Ondrea was still. He saw the old man drop to his knees. Ondrea was still. He saw Rick take the other bullets out of the gun. Ondrea was still. Sean flew out of the truck and leaped onto the back. He forcefully turned Ondrea toward him. She was in shock. He frantically examined her again and again, but she wasn't bleeding. She was not hurt. Ondrea, though she looked like a deer in headlights, was fine.

"What are you doing here?!" Sean demanded.

"I...," she whispered.

"Same thing as you." Rick was next to them now. He guided Ondrea down from the bed of the truck to the backseat. "Let's go." He signaled to Sean. Rick started the engine.

Sean watched the old man sitting on the ground, his world shaken. "What about his gun?"

Rick used his left hand to turn the wheel with a fluid motion and accelerated onto the road. "Some people shouldn't have guns."

Sean was satisfied with the answer.

*****

Rick helped Ondrea get out of the truck and gently rubbed her head. "Sean, get her in the house. I'll wait here."

Sean led Ondrea into the house. Nana B was playing with Vivi and Lilly. Like a bloodhound, she knew something was up. "What happened?" Her voice was full of concern and suspicion.

Sean stammered, "I ... we ... well..."

"I got car sick," Ondrea blurted out.

Sean glanced at Ondrea, who looked like she had just woke from a nap. He felt a lump in his throat. He swallowed hard as he followed her lead. "Rick drove a little fast after I begged him to." He paused for a moment. "Not too fast that we were in danger. But Ondrea has a sensitive stomach."

"Super sensitive." She held her stomach to be more convincing.

They both nodded.

Nana B narrowed her eyes, more on Sean than Ondrea. "Let me get you some ginger ale then." She got up from her chair and walked into the kitchen.

Sean looked back at Ondrea. "Rick wants to talk to me."

"I know."

Sean headed for the door, but heard Ondrea say, "I'm sorry."

He opened the door. "You shouldn't be. This is my fault," he said as he closed the door behind him.

Rick was waiting outside his truck, leaning against the back. Sean approached him with both of his hands in his pockets. He stopped for a second. A memory flooded his brain. He remembered getting in trouble for throwing food in the cafeteria. Walking into the house to see his father waiting in the kitchen to talk to him. His hands were so sweaty that day that they turned blue from the lining of the pockets in his school pants.

"You know what I'm going to say."

Sean shook himself awake.

"This," Rick said, emphasizing the next part, "cannot happen again."

"I know." Sean avoided eye contact.

"I mean never."

"I know."

"Do you?" Rick questioned with intensity.

Sean looked up at him.

"Ondrea could have died. Both of you could have died." Rick glared at him. He stood up and moved closer to Sean. "Look, I don't know if this–" he softened his face. "--if this is me. I mean maybe there's a reason I can't remember. Maybe I don't want to. Maybe deep down I know I don't want that life anymore."

"You've already told me this before, and then you saved Ondrea, and you were the one who said..."

"I know what I said," Rick snapped before quickly regaining his composure.

"You were the one that said you liked how it felt."

"I know that. Okay. I know what I said. Things are changing, though."

"What's changing? Are you going away again?" Sean's voice was full of panic.

"No, I'm not leaving."

"Because, if you left again..."

"Sean, I'm trying to tell you..." Rick slid his left hand through his hair holding it back for a moment. "I'm trying to tell you that I'm in love with your mother."

Sean was speechless. They stared at each other without breaking, until Ondrea suddenly stormed out of the house. She stood on the front porch with a face that neither of them could read. She marched past Sean.

"Dre?" Rick was concerned.

She searched around Rick's body. "Ondrea?" Sean called out to her. She ignored him. Then she froze with her right hand still holding onto Rick's brown, short-sleeve shirt. Ondrea gaped at Rick, who could tell from her eyes that she knew. Sean was next to them when she pulled on the hole in his shirt to show him. She let go and put her hands over her mouth. Rick took her in his arms to comfort her. It hadn't occurred to Sean that the bullet did hit someone. He realized then that Rick had saved Ondrea once again.

She gently pulled away from Rick to look at Sean, tears in her eyes. "I'm sorry."

Sean shook his head. "No, I'm the one who should be sorry."

"You tried to tell me, and I didn't..." She was wiping the tears off her cheeks, "I didn't believe you."

Sean reached out for her hand and squeezed it softly. "It wasn't like it was easy to believe." He gave her a half smile.

"I just knew something was going on." Looking now at Rick she explained, "That's why I hid in the back of your truck."

Rick was stern. "Dre." He clenched his jaw. "You know you can't tell anyone."

She wiped her face again with her hands. "No, I know. Superhero 101."

"And no more hiding in my truck... ever!" Rick was adamant.

Both nodded to him.

"I mean it."

"Everything alright?" Nana B hollered at them, holding the screen door.

"There's some napkins in the back seat, Dre."

Ondrea purposely hid her face while she went around the truck to get them.

"Yes, Nana. Everything's fine."

"I was just dropping the kids off," said Rick.

"Loretta just ran to the store. She'll be back soon if you wanna wait inside, Rick."

"That's okay, Bernadette. I have work in the morning. Can you tell her to give me a call when she gets home though?"

"Will do." She waved. "Sean, Ondrea you guys get inside and get ready for bed. You got school in the morning," Bernadette ordered.

"Coming, Nana." Sean walked off without so much as a look at Rick.

Ondrea lunged at Rick, hugging him tightly before running to catch up to Sean. Rick got into his truck but waited to make sure both kids went into the house before pulling off. Sean watched from the window as Rick's truck disappeared down the street. A feeling of defeat washed over him. Before Ondrea could turn around, Sean was running out the door.

Chapter 53

That Friday, Sean and Ondrea went to Marcus's house to finish the rest of the last Paladin comic. There were fewer people this time. Fewer children, anyway. There was also a different vibe in the house. Marcus was just as bubbly and cheerful as last time, but Maeve was nowhere to be seen. Once again, the guests were invited to sit for the reading, and once again, Marcus was delicate with the priceless artifact.

When Marcus reached the climax, Sean was shocked to hear the details about the setting. The epic battle between Paladin and Mortalan began in the Sahara Desert. He started doubting his knowledge about Paladin's end.

"'Your power will be mine!' shouted Mortalan," Marcus read.

"'I will never relinquish my power to you,' Paladin called out defiantly as he ripped the ropes that bound him in the sand."

"'I assumed as much,' Mortalan sneered. 'That's why I created the Katorein.' Mortalan advised his men to reveal what was under the grand green tarp."

Sean and Ondrea were on the edge of their seats.

"Paladin swiftly turned to see an elaborately adorned machine. Within that brief second, Mortalan had pushed the button that was in his right hand. A sudden and painful shock went through every fiber of Paladin's being. He was forced to his knees. Mortalan laughed maniacally. 'Some of us are born with power. Some of us have it thrust upon us. And some of us must fight for it. I have had to fight all my life for it.' Paladin struggled to get back to his feet. 'Your attempts are futile. The Katorein is extracting your strength from every cell of your body.' Paladin was lifted into the sky looking as helpless as a feeble child. Mortalan walked over to his sinister masterpiece, caressing it as though it was a much-loved pet. 'Then it will infuse me with your power, and I will finally become who I was always meant to be.' Without warning the Katorein began to shake uncontrollably. Mortalan's face turned pale as he desperately tried to find the issue with his grand machine. His efforts were fruitless," Marcus looked up and began to speak as if he was there. "He watched as Paladin's body was pulled closer and closer to Katorein. Once he realized that any attempt would be in vain, he understood that his only objective at that moment must be to take cover. To live to fight another day."

Ondrea leaned over to Sean and whispered, "Wow, he's really becoming the characters."

Sean was too enthralled in the story to hear her words.

"Mortalan watched from the safety of his adobe-made lair as the force of the explosion sent all of his men flying into different cardinal directions, but for Paladin," he paused for a moment reflecting on the words, "the concussive force... well, all we know is that he landed somewhere in the Pacific Ocean, never to be seen again."

Sean and Ondrea waited for Marcus to speak again, but he didn't. He just stood there, stoic, as if in another world, realm, or time.

The silence was broken by Loretta, clearing her throat.

Sean turned around to see his mother waiting to leave. He stood up. "Is that all that was written?"

"Yes." He closed the comic as tenderly as ever.

Ondrea put her hands up on top of her head. "My mind is blown right now."

"But that leaves so many questions!" Sean exclaimed.

"Yes, it does." Marcus agreed.

"Your reading was so... so... enrapturing."

Marcus' expression showed that he was impressed by the word choice.

"We have a vocabulary test coming up. She's practicing," Sean explained.

"Well, I am gratified by your flattering remark." Marcus bowed to her.

Ondrea bowed back and the three of them laughed.

"Come on guys. We have to go. I promised Rick we would be back to have dinner with him before he goes to work." Loretta grabbed Ondrea's jacket and helped her put it on.

"Before you go, I wanted to mention that I'm having brunch this Sunday with Logan Garfield."

"Logan Garfield!?" Ondrea cried out.

"Who?"

Ondrea whipped her head to Sean. "Logan Garfield. He's a reporter that focuses on the superhero universes. He's interviewed dozens of creators from Marvel, DC, Red Circle, and Dark Horse."

Marcus laughed lightly. "You certainly know your stuff. Well, if you want to join us you are more than welcome."

"Wait join you with Logan Garfield?" Ondrea asked.

"Yes, I'm inviting you and Sean," Marcus confirmed.

"Just us?" Sean inquired looking around the room.

"Maeve will be joining us."

"Just us are invited though?" Sean repeated his question

Loretta went to talk, but another girl distracted her by asking for help with her jacket zipper, which was stuck on the fabric, and as a mother, she wouldn't dare refuse.

"Well, as I mentioned Maeve will be there."

"No, I mean are we the only ones invited from the fan club?" Sean looked around the room.

"Yes, just you two." Marcus gave a small smile.

"Why?"

Marcus' smile faded a bit. "Why what?"

"Why just us?"

Marcus seemed thrown off by the question.

Ondrea elbowed Sean, but he continued anyway. "We are the newest members of the fan club. Why not pick someone like Adrian?" He gestured towards the back of the room, where Adrian stood conversing with another adolescent. "He's been a member for two years."

"Well, because you two are special. Ondrea knows more information about comics than any other adolescent I have ever met. Her knowledge isn't just focused on one or two superheroes or even one or two universes either."

Ondrea beamed.

"And you, Sean." He paused. "I have only known one other person who was as–" Marcus searched for the right word, "--obsessed with Paladin as much as you are, and that other person is standing before your eyes."

Sean looked around the room at the different kids.

"Adrian is a dedicated member and, yes, he has been for two years this December. But have you ever asked him who his favorite superhero is?"

Sean shook his head.

"It's Batman. Don't get me wrong. Batman is..."

"Awesome," Ondrea assisted.

"Yes, awesome. Thank you. But Batman is not Paladin."

Batman's not real, Sean thought to himself.

Marcus nodded at Sean as though able to hear his thoughts.

When Loretta had finally fixed the zipper, she turned back to the conversation.

"So, I hope to see you all this Sunday."

"Oh, we couldn't intrude. Also, I work Sunday so there wouldn't be anyone to drive them. Thank you, though."

"The library is closed on Sundays, mom."

Loretta, looking embarrassed, replied, "Yes, it is, but I'm volunteering at the children's wing of the Howlett Hospital starting this Sunday. I did tell you about it."

Not acknowledging that truth, Sean simply offered up a solution. "Nana B can take us."

"Sean, you don't know if she's busy."

"Well, can't we at least ask?"

"I could send a driver to pick up the children," Marcus offered.

Avoiding eye contact, Loretta responded, "Oh, I couldn't ask you to do that. I'll ask my mother to see if she's available."

"Alright then, drive safely." Marcus smiled.

"We will." Loretta ushered the kids out of the house.

Loretta unlocked the jeep, and everyone got in.

"Nana is never busy on Sundays. She says no one should work on Sundays."

"That's true. She also says it's family day." Loretta looked at him in the rearview mirror.

"It's only one Sunday, Mom."

"I know." Loretta looked back and forth between him and the road. "I'm surprised you wanna go at all. I mean, I know you wanted to finish the comic so I understood coming back one more time but that's done now."

"But we really want to meet..." Sean looked at Ondrea for help.

"Logan Garfield."

"You don't even know his name!"

"What's the reason you don't want us to go?" Sean asked.

Loretta shrugged her shoulders. "I just still think it's strange. Inviting children over for brunch. It's weird."

"He's nice. And, you know Nana won't let anything happen to us."

"I know he seems nice. I just... I don't know. Are you sure you really wanna go?"

Sean looked at Ondrea who had her hands up as if she was praying. "Yes, Mom. I want to go."

Loretta sighed, "Alright, I guess I'm out-numbered."

"So, we can go?" Ondrea asked to be sure.

Accepting defeat Loretta said, "If Nana B will take you then yes, you can go."

Ondrea hugged Sean, who blushed. Loretta, who witnessed it, smirked to herself.

Chapter 54

The next day Sean and Ondrea helped around the house more so than usual to sweeten the deal with Bernadette. They dusted, mopped, and swept the house. Larry told the kids that he would help get Bernie on board if she resisted.

"I'm sorry guys, but my book club is that day and it's my turn to host."

Ondrea and Sean were deflated.

"Well, maybe I can," Larry suggested.

"Absolutely not! The doctor said you still need to take it easy!" Bernadette was not budging.

Both kids sat at the kitchen table, drained.

"I can take them." Rick bit into an apple.

Ondrea jumped up. "Really?"

Rick nodded as he chewed.

Ondrea threw her arms around him. "Thank you, Rick!"

"No problem, Dre." He patted her back lightly.

Ondrea grabbed Sean's hand and yanked him out of his seat. "Come on. I have to teach you everything there is to know about Logan before tomorrow."

"Are you sure it's not too much trouble?" Loretta asked while touching Rick's shoulder.

He swallowed. "Not at all."

Loretta smiled with her eyes, and Rick reciprocated the look.

"Well love is certainly in the air," Bernadette announced.

"Yes, it is." Larry sat down and opened his newspaper.

"Troublemakers," Loretta commented under her breath as she sat by Larry at the table.

About an hour later, Rick knocked on Sean's open door. "Hey, can I interrupt?"

"Of course, what's up?" Ondrea closed her comic book.

"Can I borrow Sean for a bit?"

"Sure." Ondrea sprang up.

"Can it wait? Ondrea's trying to help me not embarrass myself tomorrow."

"Uh, okay then." Rick walked away.

Ondrea waited until she heard him reach the last step on the staircase. "What's that about?"

"Nothing. We're just in the zone right now." Sean managed to evade eye contact to ensure she couldn't read him. He knew what Rick wanted to say, but he wasn't ready to hear it. *The people you love are always at risk. "That's Superhero 101," Ondrea would say.* She was talking to him right now, but he couldn't hear one word. Paladin loved his mother. No, not Paladin. Rick loved his mother. Maybe Paladin really was gone. Maybe he died in that ocean that day. Sean felt his face getting hot and his legs shaking.

"Ondrea, I'm going for a run," he interrupted as he leaped from the bed.

"Is everything okay?"

He forced his feet into his sneakers. "Yes."

"Are you sure? You don't seem..."

Sean didn't stay to hear the rest of her sentence. Rick watched as Sean flew out of the screen door.

*****

Sean wasn't sure how long he had been gone. He was exhausted but didn't want to be home. He walked to the front porch and cautiously looked in one of the windows to see his mother, sister, and Rick playing the game *Trouble* together. Vivi was sitting on Rick's lap. For just a moment, Rick resembled Sean's father. Sean slumped into the armchair outside. His eyelids felt heavy. When he stopped fighting it, he quickly fell asleep.

Sean was awakened later by a cat putting her paws on his face. Vivi giggled as she forced Lilly on Sean. "She wants to give you a kiss."

Sean leaned his face to the side as the cat smelled his face and hair, and then jumped out of Vivi's hands. "Lilly, come back." She followed the cat down the porch and into the backyard.

"Hey."

Sean saw Rick sitting on the other side of him. If he hadn't spoken, he might not have noticed him at all.

"I know what you're going to say."

Rick looked to the street and back to Sean. "I wish I wasn't him."

"You're not him," Sean said plainly as he sat up.

"You're right," Rick acknowledged.

They sat there silent for some time until Ondrea came out of the house.

"I'll give you guys some privacy." Rick got up and walked to the backyard.

Ondrea moved past Sean to take Rick's chair. "Now what was that about? And don't say nothing. I know something's up with you guys."

"He doesn't want to be Paladin anymore." Sean didn't understand why, but he was fighting back tears.

"I get it. I guess this really is his hamartia."

Sean scanned the back of his brain to retrieve the meaning and when he found it, he questioned her, "How so?"

"Paladin's downfall is that he wants to be normal." Sean pondered her words as she continued. "Nothing hurts Paladin. Right? And he's not afraid of anything, but now he's happy. He has things he doesn't want to risk. Things that make him feel normal. Things he's afraid to lose. SpiderMan had Mary Jane and Aunt May. Captain America had Bucky."

Sean was biting his tongue to stop the tears from forming. "It's selfish."

Ondrea shook her head. "This may mean the end of Paladin, but I don't think he's being selfish. He really does love your mom. I think he loves all of you, honestly. I've known Rick for years, and I have never seen him with anyone. This is his family now." She paused. "It's my family now, too." She looked at him for confirmation.

Sean smiled at that statement, and Ondrea knew at once that it was true. She got up and leaned over to his side to whisper in his ear, "That doesn't make you my brother, though." Then she walked back into the house.

Sean stayed there, dizzy in a world of emotions.

Chapter 55

The car ride to Marcus' house the next day was awkward. Ondrea did her best to keep things light. She brought up subjects like the weather, school, Rick's work, Larry's recovery, Bernadette's and Loretta's cooking, Vivi, and even Lilly … anything to prevent a moment too long in silence. Sean tried to participate more, but there was a pit in his stomach that was distracting him. When the fact of the fan club was finally revealed, it was hard to tell who was more uncomfortable, Rick or Sean.

Sean got out first when they arrived.

"Dre," Rick called.

Ondrea had her door open but waited to see what Rick needed.

"Is he ever going to forgive me?"

She looked to see if Sean was within ear-shot, but he was already walking up to the house. "He's not mad at you. He's just..."

"Disappointed?"

"I... I don't know. But I know things will get better... eventually."

Rick nodded. "I think it's best if I stay out here in the car."

"Are you sure? Marcus is very welcoming."

"Yeah, the whole comic book thing isn't really for me."

"Obviously," Ondrea laughed lightly. She got out of the truck and closed the door. She jogged to catch up to Sean, who was waiting outside the door for her. Before he could knock, Maeve had opened the door.

"I thought I heard someone out here. Come in. Come in."

She seemed friendlier and more down-to-earth than before. She was even wearing jeans. The sight shocked Sean. They followed her into the dining room, where only Marcus and Logan were sitting.

"There they are." Marcus jumped out of his seat to greet them. He took the reins and guided them over to introduce them to Logan. "These are the two young fans I was talking about."

Logan, who looked like he just rolled out of bed, stood up and shook both of their hands. "Mr. Gelid was just telling me about you two."

"Please. It's Marcus, Logan."

Logan fixed his glasses, which was soon revealed to be a common mannerism. "Marcus, I mean."

"It's such an honor to meet you," Ondrea blurted out.

"The honor is all mine. I always love meeting fans of the comic world. When I was young there weren't that many of us. Where I grew up, anyway, and now we seem to be everywhere."

Ondrea was glowing.

"And you must be Sean. Marcus holds you in very high regard. I heard you're an expert."

Sean looked over at Marcus, who was smiling from ear to ear. "Well, Ondrea is the real expert."

"Not on Paladin. That's where you shine," Ondrea corrected.

"Paladin. That's one of my favorites too," said Logan.

"Everyone sit, please," Marcus insisted.

Sean looked at the chairs around the table. Logan sat by Maeve. Marcus was at the head of the table, which left two seats for Sean and Ondrea.

"Are we the only ones coming today?" Sean was still in disbelief.

"I didn't want to bombard Logan with fans." Marcus gestured them to sit.

Sean and Ondrea sat at the same time.

"Plus, we have a hidden motive for inviting you two specifically," Maeve chimed in.

Both kids looked around at the faces at the table for a clue. Marcus seemed somewhat annoyed by the reveal. In the next moment, four workers came in holding trays of croissants, mini quiches, pigs in blankets, and an array of different fruits. They laid the trays on the table. Three other workers came out with pitchers of coffee, water, and lemonade. Sean could not be sure at first, but he thought one of the servers looked very familiar to him. He searched his memory and it finally came to him. *The man from Irruption Comics.*

"Please help yourselves," Marcus insisted again.

Logan and Maeve began to fill their plates. Ondrea did the same and nudged Sean to follow her lead. Logan adjusted his glasses as he began asking the kids a variety of questions. Ondrea seemed to be in her element discussing different comic illustrators, writers, and comparing powers across the board. Sean listened. He enjoyed hearing Ondrea, as he would put it, "speak comics." The first hour flew by, but Sean started feeling uneasy. The idea of a secret agenda was nagging at him. He would glance over, but Marcus didn't seem to notice. Finally, Sean mustered up the courage during an opening in the conversations to ask, "So what is your hidden motive?"

The question appeared to sit there in the air for a moment. Marcus cleared his throat, "I'm so sorry, this must have been gnawing at you this entire time. Well, before I answer that, let me say first, that I am getting older, as you all can see."

The words made Sean realize that Marcus was looking older. His hair was noticeably grayer, and his face seemed thinner. It was odd because the change had transpired over a little more than a week. Sean wondered how such a transformation could occur so rapidly.

Marcus continued, "The truth is I want to pursue other avenues in my life. It was my plan to be the president of this fan club for a brief time. That plan has been extended on several occasions." Marcus smiled at Maeve, who only nodded in return. "I guess I felt it was my duty to keep the position until I found the right individual to take my place."

Sean realized that everyone was looking at him. "Wait, you mean me. But I'm only twelve." He lowered his eyebrows, almost outraged.

"Well, yes, but that is why I also wanted to make Ondrea vice president."

Ondrea, who had just taken a bite of her croissant, smiled, forcing the food to look like a bubble on the side of her face.

"And, of course, Maeve will look over the major responsibilities until you feel comfortable to take over completely." Maeve bowed her head to them as if to say, at your service.

Logan pushed his glasses up. "That's why I'm here. I'm documenting the shift of titles."

"Precisely," Marcus said. Then one of the servants walked over to him and whispered something in his ear. Whatever it was it seemed to make Marcus eager, and Maeve intrigued.

"That seems kinda beneath you," Ondrea remarked to Logan without thinking. "I mean no disrespect though."

Logan, before answering, looked over to ensure their conversation was not being monitored. "None taken. The truth is Maeve's family is a big contributor to Comicverse and my editor likes to keep all of our contributors happy."

"You work a lot with Maeve?" Sean inquired.

"Oh God no." Logan was now whispering. "I mean don't get me wrong, she can be very..." He scanned his brain for the right words.

"Disturbing," Sean assisted without blinking.

"Well, I wouldn't phrase it that way exactly." Logan chuckled. "No, I don't see her often. Most of her energy is focused on Irruption Comics."

Sean knew at that moment he was right about the servant. He had seen him before, and it was at Irruption Comics. Sean remembered that day. He remembered the eerie feeling of being watched while he was there. He had that same feeling again as his eyes shot up and met Maeve's.

The worker had now left to the other room. "So, what do you say?" Marcus placed his elbows on the table and folded his hands together. When no response was given, Marcus pressed, "Sean, tell us your answer?"

Sean couldn't make sense of it one way or another, so he answered honestly, "I'm sorry, but I'm just not sure."

Everyone froze at hearing Sean's reply. Even the workers were at a halt in their steps and duties. A silence had taken hold of the room. Ondrea was the only one that dared to break it. "I think Sean needs some time to think it over."

"Think it over?" Maeve mimicked. "What is there to think over?" It seemed that she had been restraining herself this entire time, but in that moment, her mask had fallen. Sean had forgotten how cold her voice could sound. Marcus laid his hand on Maeve's wrist, and she immediately regained her composure. He seemed to have a power over her. A power that mystified Sean.

"Of course. Discuss it and let me know when you have an answer for me," Marcus proposed.

"I will. We will." Sean glanced over at Ondrea, giving her the signal that it was time to go.

Reading Sean's body language as well, Marcus took his napkin off his lap and placed it onto his plate as he said, "Let me escort you two out." He stood up and then walked around the table. Logan shot up while wiping his hands with his napkin to shake Sean and Ondrea's hands. "It was truly a pleasure talking to you guys today."

"The pleasure was all ours," Ondrea marveled.

"It was very nice to meet you," Sean added.

Rick was outside his truck smoking a cigarette. He tossed it when he saw the kids coming.

"Thought you quit?" Ondrea whispered to him.

"Trying," he mumbled under his breath.

"Is this your father?" Marcus asked, wide-eyed.

"No, he's..." Sean was unsure what to call him.

"He's Rick," Ondrea rang in.

"Nice to meet you." Rick offered his hand.

Marcus accepted. "Well, it's nice to meet you also, Rick."

"Alright, you guys good to go?" He looked at both kids for confirmation.

"Thanks again for coming over for brunch," Marcus said. "And Sean, you'll let me know when you've made your decision."

Sean nodded as he opened the back door of the truck to climb in.

"Thanks for having us," Ondrea called out from her window.

"It was a pleasure as always." Marcus waved.

"I didn't catch your name."

"Call me Marcus."

"Alright, Marcus." They shook hands again.

As they drove off, Rick looked in his rear-view mirror and saw Marcus standing next to someone.

"Is that his wife?"

Both kids turned around.

"No, that's Maeve. She's actually the daughter of Bao Eldritch," Ondrea explained.

"Who?"

"The creator of your comic book, Paladin." Ondrea rolled her eyes playfully.

"Oh, right."

Ondrea switched her attention to Sean. "So, what are you thinking?"

"I have a lot going on with school and home."

"I live with you now, remember. I know you don't have that much going on. And, I would be the vice president. I would help you with everything."

Sean looked at Ondrea but didn't respond.

"A month ago you would have jumped at this chance."

"Things are different now," Sean muttered as he looked up at the rear-view mirror, but all he could see were Rick's sunglasses. He wasn't sure whether his comment was heard. Rick felt it was better that way and focused on his driving.

Chapter 56

An entire week went by, but Sean was still putting off his decision. That Saturday, Larry watched a Rolls Royce pull up in the driveway. The driver stepped out to open the door for Marcus, who immediately put on a pair of very small and round sunglasses. He stepped up to the house and addressed Larry, "Hello sir, I am Marcus Gelid. President..."

"I know who you are, sir. Word travels fast around here and I'm pretty good at putting two and two together."

Marcus gave a small smile.

"The kids are in the backyard playing. Let me walk you over." After a small struggle, Larry was up and walking. He escorted Marcus to the back of the house where Sean was sitting watching Rick, Ondrea, and Vivi play with a Nerf football.

"Sean, this fella was looking for you."

"Marcus, um." Sean jumped off the back porch step. "Hi, what are you doing here?"

"Well, I was in the neighborhood so I figured I would drop in and see if you were any closer to making a decision."

"Hi, Marcus," Ondrea huffed, trying to catch her breath.

"Hello, Ondrea and ... Rick?" Marcus pointed.

"That's right." Rick had Vivi on his shoulders.

"And who is this little one?"

"I'm Vivi."

"No, you're trouble," Rick joked as he tickled Vivi. Her laughter made the others smile.

Loretta came out of the back door holding a tray of lemonade. Rick put Vivi down to help Loretta.

"Thanks, Honey." Loretta rubbed his back. Rick laid the tray on a small table that had a large umbrella to shade the area, and Loretta began pouring. "Larry, is Mom back yet?"

"No, not yet."

Loretta turned and finally noticed that they had company. "Oh, Mr. Gelid. What a ... pleasant surprise. Would you like a glass of lemonade?"

"No, I would hate to trouble you. Besides, I am not staying long. I just wanted to see if my young fan here has made up his mind yet."

Sean felt like all eyes were on him again, but really it was just Ondrea and Marcus.

"I'm sorry, but I'm still thinking about it."

Ondrea looked disappointed until Marcus suggested, "What if we do a trial basis?"

"Trial basis?"

"A kind of probation period. You try the hat on, wear it for a bit, and then decide if you want to keep it. How does that sound?"

"That sounds like a good idea to me," Ondrea chimed in.

"Uh, yeah. Okay," Sean agreed.

"Well, then it's settled." Marcus clapped his hands together holding them for a second.

"When do we start?" Ondrea asked eagerly.

"Tomorrow."

"Tomorrow?" Both Ondrea and Sean repeated with very different connotations.

"How high?" Rick was heard in the background.

"So, so, so, so high," Vivi said.

"So, so, so, so high?" Rick echoed.

Vivi nodded in an exaggerated manner.

"Yes, tomorrow. I will bring over all the paperwork that explains the responsibilities of the president and vice president. Around this time good?" Marcus asked.

"Uh, yeah it should be," said Sean.

"Tomorrow then." Marcus gave a slight bow with his head and began walking away slowly.

"Alright, so, so, so, so high, coming right up." Rick wound his left arm up and threw the football.

"That was so high. Where'd it go? I can't see it." Vivi squinted her eyes at the sky.

Everyone followed Vivi's lead searching for the missing football in the clouds.

Loretta had one hand over her brow trying to see. "Where did it go?" she questioned.

Even Marcus stopped and turned around to watch the show.

"There it is." Rick caught a glimpse of the blue and yellow toy coming down, then caught the ball with one hand.

Marcus soon realized that Sean was looking at him. "See you tomorrow," he reminded Sean with a smile as he continued to his car.

"That was strange," Ondrea said to Sean as Marcus exited.

"I think he's just lonely."

"No, not that. He was acting different." She looked perplexed.

"What do you mean?"

"I don't know. Just–" She turned her mouth to the side."--seemed older today to me. Ya know. He was walking slower and even when he spoke it just seemed like…," she put her shoulders up. "…different. Marcus said he was getting older but maybe he's actually sick or something."

Sean reflected on her words.

Loretta broke his train of thought. "So, are you the president now?"

"Only trying it out for a while," Ondrea said.

"To see if I like it." Sean walked over to the table.

"Well, at least that explains it all." Loretta took a sip of her lemonade.

"Explains what?" Sean asked as he sat down.

"Why Mr. Gelid seemed so–" Loretta paused. "--preoccupied with you guys. He was just…"

"Vetting us," Ondrea finished her sentence. "He had to make sure we would be right for the job." She sat in a chair next to Sean.

"That's an excellent word to describe it," Loretta said.

Ondrea glowed. "I guess he deemed us worthy."

"I guess so." Loretta offered lemonade to Ondrea, who graciously accepted it.

Chapter 57

Every Sunday, Marcus came over for two hours to explain the responsibilities and perks of the president and vice president. Every time Marcus looked and acted a bit older. On their last encounter, which was Halloween, Rick had to help escort him to his car. Sean and Ondrea didn't know what to make of it.

"Maybe Ondrea's right. Maybe he is sick, and he can't be president," Loretta suggested, as they began walking the streets, trick or treating.

"And maybe he doesn't want anyone to know he's sick," Ondrea added.

Sean tried to focus on the conversation but kept getting distracted by Ondrea's Catwoman costume. Her long black hair was curled at the ends and somehow her different-colored eyes shined brighter beneath the mask. Vivi was holding Ondrea's hand and informed everyone that since she was a cat and Ondrea was Cat-woman that they must stick together for the rest of the night. Sean was dressed like Luke Skywalker since he was not allowed to go with his first pick, which was Michael Myers.

When Rick caught up to them, he announced that Marcus had requested that from now on they meet at his house instead.

"Really? Another Sunday? What's left to still go over?" Loretta questioned Sean.

"Mom, you just said he might be sick. Maybe he just likes the company."

Loretta looked proud, even more so in her Audrey Hepburn costume. "You're right. That was wrong of me."

"Why are you looking at me like that?"

"I'm just impressed, that's all."

"Mom, stop. Please."

"Alright, alright." Loretta turned to Rick, who had conveniently forgotten to buy a cos-tume. "I can't take them next week. I prom-ised the kids at Howlett that I'd finish reading *Charlotte's Web* to them. I hate asking you to, but..."

"You know I don't mind. It's my day off anyway."

"That's why I hate asking you. It's your only day off from both jobs."

Rick grabbed her hand to kiss it. "No worries. I'll take them."

They shared a loving glare until Sean cleared his throat.

"Oh wow, look at those decorations." Loretta signaled to a house with fake spider webs, black cats, and witches surrounding the lawn.

"Mommy, can we go there?" Vivi asked.

"Of course, Lovebug."

Vivi grabbed her mother's hand, yanking her from Rick, while still holding on to Ondrea's. "Come on. Let's go."

Rick chuckled. "She can be quite demanding when she wants to be, huh?"

"You have no idea." Sean began walking away to follow them then turned back to Rick. "When are you telling her that you love her?"

"Who? Bernadette? I don't need to say it, she already knows."

"I'm serious."

"I can see that." Rick stepped closer to Sean and exhaled hard. "Look, the truth is. I already told your mom."

Sean twisted his candy bag around and around, then back the other way.

Rick tucked his hands into the pockets of his jeans. "She didn't say it back."

Sean's eyes shot up at Rick. He was both surprised and glad. "It's probably for the best."

"Why do you say that?" Rick tried not to look bothered.

"I was thinking about it the other day. How old are you?" Sean did not wait for an answer. "You look like you're in your forties, but we both know that's not true."

Rick folded his arms on his chest as he said, "Alright. I know what you're getting at."

"Have you even thought about it?" Sean's tone was getting firmer. "She'll continue to age while you stay like this. My mom wants someone to grow old with. And that's something you can't do for her." Rick was silent as he stared at the ground. Sean knew it was wrong to kick a man when he was down, but he proceeded anyway. "Maybe this is something you should consider. Ya know, before it's too late."

Ondrea and Loretta waved to them to hurry up. Sean caught up quickly, but Rick was slower now, carrying a much heavier weight upon his shoulders.

Chapter 58

Rick was hardly over the next month. He even missed Thanksgiving dinner. He said he was tired from working overtime. Soon it was a cold December for everyone, but especially Loretta. She worried that Rick wasn't being completely honest when he told her nothing was wrong. He sounded like a different person on the phone. And the only time he came over was to take the kids to Marcus' house, strategically after Loretta had left for the hospital. Sean's words had penetrated the great Rick. Sean knew they did, and he told himself that he had done the right thing, though the mirror said otherwise.

When the next Sunday came round, Loretta was running late. Rick was reluctant to go to the door when he saw her jeep still parked, but not seeing another alternative, he knocked.

"Hey, stranger." Loretta tried to sound light as she opened the door.

"Hey." Rick, without removing his sunglasses, leaned in to give her a peck on her cheek. "Heading to the hospital?"

"Yeah, I'm already late." Loretta looked up at him. "Will I see you for dinner tonight?"

"I have work early tomorrow, so I'm just going to pick up something after I drop the kids back here, then head to bed."

Loretta's eyes hit the ground. She bit her lip to hold back the emotions that were coming to the surface. "Okay, I get it." She took a deep breath and looked up at him again. "You know you don't have to take them anymore."

"I promised I would." Rick was avoiding eye contact. His eyes were shielded, but they were still powerless if they looked into hers.

They lingered there in the doorway for a moment. Loretta cleared her throat. "Well, I should go." Rick stepped out of her way to let her pass. "See you guys tonight," she called back to the others. Loretta walked over to her jeep. She looked back one more time before getting in, but Rick wasn't facing her. He hadn't been for some time.

Rick waited to hear her car leave before he spoke again. "You guys ready?"

"I'll get Ondrea." Sean ran up the stairs.

"Ya know you can come in, Rick." Bernadette made her way over to him.

Rick shook his head. "Better if I stay out here."

"Everything alright, Rick?" Bernadette folded her arms and tilted her head to the right.

"Yes ma'am. I'm…," he paused for a moment. "Can you tell the kids I'll be in the truck?"

"I can do that."

Rick walked off. Ondrea and Sean came stomping down the stairs.

"Hey. Hey. Take it easy on this old house."

"Sorry, Bernadette." Ondrea flew out the door.

Sean was getting his jacket off the hook to do the same.

"Sean?"

"Sorry, Nana. I know. Save my running for outside."

"Yes, please do. But before you go, can you tell me what's going on?"

Sean shrugged his shoulders. "We're going to Marcus'. Rick's taking us." He put one sleeve on.

"Not about that. You saw what I saw with your mother and Rick. Now stop playing coy and tell me what's going on."

"How would I know?" Sean looked outside to press the point that he needed to leave.

"I think you do know. I even think you played a part in it, especially since you haven't looked me in the eyes."

"I don't know what you want me to say, Nana." Sean put the other sleeve on and adjusted the hood.

Ondrea popped her head back into the house. "What's taking so long, Sean?"

"I got to go, okay?" Sean finally looked at his grandmother.

"We'll finish this conversation soon." Bernadette gave a stern look that made Sean shudder inside.

Sean felt himself struggle as he walked out of the house. He hadn't felt this guilty before.

He had justified separating his mother and Rick. Now he was questioning his true intentions behind it. Was he just being spiteful? Was he holding resentment because he didn't get what he wanted? Only his Nana had this kind of power, he thought.

Chapter 59

Sean could not remember a thing about the drive to Marcus' that day. He was lost trying to find his thoughts in the snow. Ondrea had to shake him as if he was sleeping when they arrived. Marcus was outside waiting for them with Maeve and a little boy, no more than five years old.

"Who's that little boy with them?" Ondrea looked out the window.

"No idea," Sean answered honestly.

"Marcus looks worse."

Sean agreed, "He's going to need a wheel-chair soon."

Everyone got out of the truck.

"Hello, all. I'm so glad that you were able to make the trip through the snow." Marcus waved them over.

The little boy ran straight to Rick insisting to be picked up. Rick scooped him up with his left hand. "Who's this little guy?"

"This is my son, Arjun," Maeve said.

"I didn't know you had a son," Ondrea blurted out loudly and then blushed.

"Well, I do my best to keep him out of my work life." Maeve took him from Rick's arms.

The boy resembles Bao when he was young, Sean thought as he recalled the photo in the newspaper.

"Let's move this gathering to the backyard. I have a surprise for you guys." Marcus gestured with his cane.

"What kind of surprise?" asked Ondrea.

"You'll see."

Ondrea tagged Sean on the shoulder. "Come on, slowpoke."

Sean chased after her. Rick stood still as the others moved forward. Marcus stopped in his tracks, "You as well, Rick." Without waiting for a response, he continued, "I will not have a guest sitting in a truck in this cold weather again."

Rick, not wanting to be rude, started to follow behind them. To the amazement of all the guests, the large lake behind Marcus' house was covered in ice.

"Would you kids enjoy skating today?"

"But we don't have skates with us," Ondrea answered, disappointed.

"I think you will find your size over there." Marcus signaled to a large box that was not far from where they were standing. The kids ran over to it and found multiple pairs of ice skates. Ondrea found her size right away. Sean found his at the bottom of the box. Arjun managed to escape his mother's grasp. She attempted again to catch him, but Marcus held his hand up and Maeve obeyed. Only Rick witnessed this strange interaction. Ondrea came running up holding her skates. "Marcus, can I please use your bathroom before we skate?"

"Of course. Be my guest. Do you remember where it is?"

Ondrea nodded as she put her skates down, then struggled through the snow as she ran to the house.

"Are you going to skate as well? We merely approximated the sizes, but we have a pair that we believe will fit you," Marcus said to Rick.

"That's kind of you, but I'm not much of a skater. I'm not even sure his mother would want them to skate either." Rick put his hands to his mouth to magnify his voice. "Hey, Sean!"

"I can assure you that the lake is perfectly safe. Arjun was skating on it just yesterday." Marcus motioned to Maeve to agree and once again she complied.

"Please, let's sit and chat while the children have their fun."

The three adults sat at a bench that was conveniently placed on the solid ground facing the lake.

Rick, unable to ignore his gut feeling, shot up to his feet. "Let me just check that the kids are allowed to skate."

"By all means, if it will settle your nerves." Marcus smiled.

Rick walked over to Sean.

"I know you are not happy about this, but we must test our theory," Marcus whispered to Maeve.

Ondrea came out of the house at that moment and found a path to follow that was paved from the snow. It led straight to the bench.

Ondrea was now within earshot, unbeknown to Marcus and Maeve.

"We both know that I am running out of time."

Maeve remained reserved, staring out at the ice.

"I am trying to keep my promise to you."

"He's only five years old," Maeve hissed.

"You do not need to remind me of the child's age," Marcus said through his teeth.

Ondrea purposely stepped into the snow on the side of the walking path to announce her presence.

Both Maeve and Marcus turned to look at her at once.

She forced a smile. "Can't wait to get on that ice."

"I bet." Marcus' features softened.

Ondrea stood there frozen like the water in the lake.

"Well, you better hurry up before it melts," Marcus teased.

Ondrea laughed awkwardly while jogging back to the others.

"I've skated before. My mom was the one who taught me how. Trust me she won't mind." Sean walked cautiously to the ice dismissing Rick's concerns and began to glide across the lake.

"Hey, you're not gonna even wait for me?" Ondrea called out as she rushed to change into her skates.

"Hurry up, slowpoke," Sean said as he sailed from one side to the other.

Rick assisted Arjan in tying his laces. When he was finished helping, Arjan grabbed his hand and said, "Thank you, take me to the ice, please." Ondrea walked with them. Rick was impressed by how well Arjan skated for his age. He stood there watching guard as the three kids enjoyed the nature-made rink until Marcus summoned him back to the bench.

"So, how long have you lived in Virginia?"

"Around ten years."

"And where did you live before that?"

"Alaska."

"Alaska," Marcus repeated. He looked as if a light had just been turned on in his head. Unable to help his curiosity he attempted to continue his inquisition. "You were born there?"

Rick gave him a slightly suspicious look.

Maeve jumped up as she witnessed Arjan fall. "Arjan, are you okay?" The little boy nodded and was up on his skates again with Sean's help, but Maeve continued to stand there with the same worried expression upon her face.

"I'm terribly sorry. I know I'm asking too many questions. Just trying to make conversation." Marcus chuckled.

Rick was also keeping his focus on the children but quickly answered, "I'm not sure, to be honest. I was in a boating accident."

Marcus' eyes brightened and for a moment he looked like his old young self until Maeve interrupted. "I think Arjan has had enough. I'm going to call him in."

Rick was confused by their bizarre relationship. He wondered why she was asking for his permission when Arjan was her son, but he put it out of his head, reminding himself that it was none of his business.

"Maeve, you're such a worrier."

"I have a bad feeling, okay?"

"You're going to make him weak." Marcus emphasized the last word as he stared dead-locked into Maeve's eyes. Rick was once again distracted by the peculiar connection between the two of them. The powerful gaze seemed to paralyze Maeve until a loud scream released her. Rick realized instantly what took the others longer to figure out.

Without hesitation, Rick jumped into action. In a flash, he was on the ice commanding Sean and Ondrea to get off the lake. Maeve passed the other two children as she finally made a decision of her own accord. She was ungraceful in her black boots on the slippery surface but was determined to get to her son. It only took Rick three seconds to find where Arjan had floated under the ice, and only one punch from Rick's left hand to break through near Arjan. Then Rick tore off his coat and submerged the upper half of his body into the frigid water. Within the next second, he freed Arjan from the cold prison and imminent death. He held the little boy close to him as he carried him back to his mother's arms. Maeve's eyes were filled with tears as she rushed his tiny, soaking wet body into the house with Rick following behind. Sean and Ondrea hurried to take off their skates. Once they switched to their boots, they bolted to the house. Maeve had undressed Arjan down to his car briefs and put him into a giant red towel. He was shaking and his lips were blue.

"Please help him," she begged Rick.

Rick put his hands diagonally across his stomach and lifted his soaking wet sweater off from the bottom up revealing a white tank top underneath. He held out his hands to take Arjan. Maeve hesitated, but only for a second. Sean and Ondrea appeared in the doorway to see Rick holding Arjan in his arms. The little boy was no longer shaking. Tears were rolling down Maeve's cheeks as she held her son's little hand to her mouth. The sight made Ondrea cry as well. Sean put his arm around her to console her when he saw Marcus out of the corner of his eye in the window. He was still sitting on the bench outside facing the lake, immune to and untouched by the events happening.

Time seemed to stand still, and no one there could say how much time actually passed. Then a little voice was heard. "Mommy, I'm hungry."

At the sound of those words, Maeve let out a sigh of relief. She gently took Arjan from Rick. "What would you like Mommy to make you?" Maeve did not utter a word to Rick, but her eyes said thank you a thousand times. Rick nodded in acknowledgment.

"I want mac and cheese," Arjan answered as he rested his head on his mother's chest.

"Mac and cheese it is then." Maeve held him in one hand and used the other to fill a pot with water, place it on the stove, and turn the burner on high. While the water was heating up, she sat at the table in the kitchen holding her son close and humming a tune in his ear. Sean was surprised at how maternal she looked.

Marcus came into the house at that moment. "I've sent for my physician to come and make a house call to check on Arjan."

Maeve did not acknowledge any of his words or his presence. She just continued humming to Arjan.

Rick picked up his wet sweater. "I think we should leave now."

"I hope not. There are still so many questions I have for you... Paladin."

At first, Sean was sure that he had imagined hearing the name until he saw Ondrea and Rick's expressions.

A man walked in holding a sweater and gave it to Marcus, who said, "Thank you. Please retrieve Mr. Neige's coat." The servant nodded. Marcus gestured to Rick to take the sweater. "Not that you need it. I bet your body temperature never dropped below ninety-eight degrees."

It was true. Rick did not feel the cold, but he took the sweater to put on because he felt exposed, in more ways than one.

"It really was a heroic feat back there. Maybe Marcus is right. We should nickname you 'Paladin.'" Ondrea forced an awkward laugh.

"Please, Miss Mirk. Don't insult me." Marcus walked into the dining room and the three of them followed. Rick placed his large hands on a chair that was set at the table. Marcus picked up a copy of a Paladin comic that was nearby. It was the eighth issue titled *Paladin: In the Blood*. He glanced back and forth between the cover and Rick as he spoke, "I wasn't sure at first. When I saw you, I did not see him. Slowly though, through each encounter we have had, more and more I became convinced. And, after today, well, I would wager my life on it." He placed the comic book back.

Despite all their issues, Sean found himself feeling protective over Rick. "What do you want from him?" Sean demanded.

"My dear boy, it's not what I want from him. It's what I can do for him."

Rick remained silent as Marcus went on. "What if I told you that there was a way to stop being Paladin? Not just ignoring who you were, but…" He spoke slowly and deliberately now. "Permanently and completely becoming who you are now. To truly be Patrick Neige."

"How do you know so much about…," Ondrea paused for a moment to consider what to call him. "Rick?"

"He's been watching him this whole time," Sean answered for Marcus.

"You're very perceptive, Mr. O'Leary." Marcus nodded. "It's true. I've done my homework."

"Is the fan club even real?" Ondrea asked, feeling betrayed.

"Yes, my dear. The fan club is very real and also the most effective way to find the real Paladin. Don't get me wrong. We've gone down many roads thinking we were on the right path, only to wind up at a dead end. Many close calls. But, in the end, none of them could hold a candle to the great Paladin." Marcus breathed in deeply. "I have found you though. Finally, I have found you."

"Who are you... really?" Sean narrowed his eyes and tightened his fists.

"Just an old admirer of our noble hero."

Ondrea spoke directly to Rick, "I think we should go now."

"Aren't you even curious?" Marcus' body might have been feeble, but his eyes were full of strength.

Rick looked up at Marcus and then at Ondrea. He saw the fear growing in her eyes. Rick was beyond curious to hear Marcus out, but once again his heroic instincts kicked in. "Come on, kids. Let's go." He walked by Marcus and growled, "You can keep the coat."

The three of them walked out of the house together. Before he entered the truck, Sean turned to see Marcus standing at the top of the stairs. He wore not a look of defeat, but one of satisfaction upon his weathered face. The sight told Sean things were far from over.

Chapter 60

During the entire drive home, Ondrea was babbling. She went in circles and back around about how they should have never trusted Marcus, how foolish she felt, and how Loretta was right from the beginning. What she said next caught Sean and Rick's attention.

"I still feel kinda bad for him, though." Sean looked at her as she continued. "I overheard him talking to Maeve about not having much time left. I really do believe he's dying. Maybe meeting Paladin was his final wish before, ya know, he goes."

Rick was silent. Ondrea looked to Sean for some sort of stability in the madness.

"I don't know," was all he managed to say.

Rick dropped them off without moving from the driver's seat.

"Aren't you coming in?" Ondrea asked as she got out.

"No, I have some things I need to do."

Sean knew it was a lie but didn't press. He figured Rick was avoiding his mother. Besides, Sean wanted to run. He had been holding it in since Marcus first addressed Rick as Paladin. They watched Rick drive off.

Ondrea turned to Sean. "Go ahead."

He looked at her and she repeated herself. She had become quite keen on reading the signs that indicated he needed a run.

"Don't be too long, though. We need to talk more, and we still have math homework to finish."

"Okay," he responded as he took off. He ran around the school and found himself passing Rick's place. Sean squinted his eyes to make out the sight before him. Rick was sitting in his truck, stoic. He looked like he had more than the weight of the world on his shoulders. Sean suddenly felt that weight as well. He had pushed his mother and Rick together, and now he had pushed them apart. He had introduced Marcus into his life and the ramifications of this were yet to be seen.

Rick stayed there, stagnant in his own purgatory. Sean couldn't get himself to run anymore. He walked the rest of the way back home. He didn't know how to fix things. He planted the seed that had now grown out of his control. *Ondrea will know how to fix this*, the thought allowed him to feel more at ease. For a moment he felt like things could go back to the way they were with her help. The feeling faded away as he saw three men talking to Nana B, Larry, and his mother. The first two men were police officers and the third man he recognized as Ondrea's lawyer, Mr. Richards. He was balding in the back and was just a shade darker than Larry.

As Sean approached, he heard Mr. Richards say, "Ondrea's family." Sean felt his heart sink. He didn't know what Mr. Richards wanted or needed from Ondrea, but he knew in his gut from the way his mother looked over at him that it was going to hurt.

"I think it's best we talk to her first, don't you think?" Nana B wasn't really asking.

Mr. Richards reflected on her words. "Yes, that might be best. This is a delicate matter. You can understand why Ms. Nesta is eager to see her, though."

"Yes, I can understand that. Let me speak with her first though and then I will call you."

Nana B was respectful but adamant in her tone.

"Well, you have my card."

"I do." Nana B put out her hand to shake his. "Thank you, Mr. Richards."

He shook hands with Loretta and Larry before leaving.

"You talk to Sean, and I'll speak to Ondrea?" Nana B suggested.

Loretta nodded. Larry followed Bernadette back into the house saying, "I think it's a good night to barbecue, Bernie."

"In this weather, you're crazy."

"It's not that cold."

"There's snow on the ground."

"Barely," Larry mumbled.

"Alright, but you're on your own." Their voices faded to the background.

"Hey. We need to talk." Loretta gestured to the chairs on the front porch.

Sean sat silently as he tried to follow everything his mother said. She told him how Nana B had looked into adopting Ondrea so that she could stay with them permanently. How, apparently, some kind of flag went up when she did. And how Ondrea's father had changed their last name illegally to hide her from her aunt, who had been desperately searching for her all these years after her sister's death.

Ondrea lost her mother. She never told me. Sean always felt that Ondrea understood his pain. The pain that changed him. The pain that made him run. The pain from the loss of his father. It never occurred to him that the reason could be because she experienced that pain as well. "How long has she been looking for her?"

"Mr. Richards said it was over ten years now."

They had stayed there for some time quiet before Sean mustered the strength to ask, "So Ondrea is leaving then?"

"I'm sorry, Sean, but I'm not sure." Loretta leaned over and placed one hand on top of Sean's holding it gently.

Sean felt his throat closing and his eyes watering. He shot up and started to run away. He made it to the mailbox before he heard the screen door swing open. He stopped in his tracks to see Ondrea standing there. In the next second, he was running back. He was running to her. And she ran to him. Halfway, they found each other and held on as tightly as they could. Nana B ushered Loretta and Larry away to give them some privacy.

"You don't have to go. We can fight this," Sean whispered in her ear. "We can fight this."

Ondrea pulled away enough to reveal tears in her eyes. "I want to meet her." She bit her lip. "I need to meet her."

Though Sean wasn't running anymore his heart was still racing. He looked away from her for a moment, staring at the street and then back to her. Her gaze made him breathe heavily. He felt the adrenaline entering his bloodstream. Before Sean could talk himself out of it, he pressed his lips against hers. It was a soft delicate kiss that made him feel faint. Seconds later, Ondrea jerked herself away and ran back into the house. Sean was left there standing alone.

Chapter 61

Bernadette made good on her promise to call Mr. Richards back. They set up a meeting for the very next day. Ondrea didn't come down for dinner that night. She told Nana B that she was going to bed early. Larry was disappointed, but he made sure to save her plate, just in case. She was still sleeping when Sean got up to get ready. His mother informed him that Ondrea would be missing school that day to meet her aunt.

Not having Ondrea at school was more of a distraction to Sean than if she had been there. The day felt like an eternity. When the last bell finally rang, to his astonishment, he didn't rush out the doors like the rest of the kids did. He was scared to face what might be true. Eventually, Sean walked outside to see his mother waiting for him, holding Vivi in her arms.

"Where's the jeep?"

"I thought it might be nice to walk home since it was a bit warmer today. The snow's been cleared, so it won't be hard."

Sean's steps still felt cumbersome even without the snow. Loretta placed Vivi down to walk. He was expecting a long talk from his mother, but it was Vivi who did most of the talking. She told him all about her day at school. How Mrs. Grey, her pre-K teacher, had become a scientist. That she put on a white coat and a funny white wig. That she put a balloon on a bottle, and how the bottle blew into the balloon and the balloon became big. Then she spoke about how during nap time, Esequiel kept giggling for no reason, and how it made everyone else giggle except Raven, who didn't think it was funny. Vivi told him how their mother forgot to put her favorite snack, Goldfish, in her lunchbox, but that Mrs. Grey shared some of hers, so it was okay. Sean took in every word, smile, and laugh of his sister. By the time they got to the house, Sean was feeling a little better.

He walked into the living room to see Ondrea sitting next to a woman that strongly resembled her. She even had the two different colored eyes like Ondrea, but not as pretty if you asked Sean. It was obvious from both of their faces that they had been crying.

"You must be Sean. Ondrea has told me so much about you. I'm Eirene." She stood up to show that she was not much taller than Ondrea.

"This is my aunt, Sean."

Sean shook her hand. "It's nice to meet you."

"Alright, well. I have a lot of arrangements to make so I better be going." Eirene hugged Ondrea and began to cry again. "I'm so happy, Ondrea."

"I am too." Her voice cracked.

Eirene released Ondrea and wiped her eyes as she said, "Okay, no more tears." She wiped Ondrea's as well. She gave her another hug. "I'll pick you up around five on Wednesday."

At those words, Sean's world sank. Eirene shook hands with everyone else and thanked them tremendously for their hospitality to her, and especially to Ondrea. It wasn't until she left that everyone noticed Sean was gone as well. Usually, everyone just waited for Sean to come back from his runs, but Nana B decided to take action this time. She drove up beside him in Larry's pick-up truck. "Come on, let's go. I need to help your mother with dinner."

Sean got in without protesting because he knew it was a battle he would not win.

As usual, Bernadette wasted no time. She dove right in with, "I know you know she's leaving."

Sean did not respond.

"I know that's hard on you. It's hard on all of us. Though, I know it's hardest on you."

Sean remained silent.

"But you are wasting the time you have with her."

The words hit Sean hard. He closed his eyes from the pain. "I don't want her to go."

"I know you don't." She hesitated for a moment. "But sometimes we think things will be worse than they actually are." She pulled the truck into the driveway, but they didn't get out.

"I don't even know where she's going."

Bernadette, wanting to be transparent with Sean, admitted, "Her aunt lives in Pennsylvania."

Sean stared at her, appalled. "How could things be worse?"

"Honestly." She looked him directly in the eyes. "She could still be living with her father."

Sean knew his grandmother was right. He looked up at the house to see Ondrea standing on the porch waiting for him.

"I'm not gonna lie and say this won't be hard. But it's not impossible." She pulled him over to her and kissed his head. "Now, get out."

Sean obeyed the order and stepped out of the car to meet Ondrea. They were inseparable for the next forty-eight hours. Loretta allowed them to sleep in the same room if that room was the living room, and Vivi could join them. That Tuesday night, they laid there in sleeping bags facing each other on the living room floor, with Vivi in the middle asleep.

"Ondrea, I want to tell you..."

"Don't. Don't tell me now," she interrupted. "Wait until tomorrow."

"Why?"

"I don't think I'm ready to hear it yet."

Sean understood.

Ondrea changed the subject. "Ya know, something's been bothering me since we left Marcus' house the other day."

"What is it?"

"How much of that day do you think was planned? The skates were there in our sizes. Arjun was there for the first time. I mean we never met him before, and then out of nowhere he's there to be...," she paused, "saved?"

Sean pondered her words. "Are you saying Marcus planned for Arjun to fall in? You really think Maeve would let him do that?"

"I don't know," she yawned. "I'm not sure if he could have planned Arjan falling in, but he knew Rick was coming, and he knew who Rick was, or is, or was. I don't know. It just seems weird, right?"

Sean tried to think about it more, but he was slowly fading into sleep.

Ondrea saw his eyes getting heavy and decided to drop the subject. "Nevermind." She yawned again. "Goodnight, Sean."

"Goodnight." He reached his hand out to her and she held it. Soon, they were both fast asleep.

Chapter 62

The next day was difficult for everyone. Larry, though, voiced his concerns and opinions louder than anyone else. "It doesn't make any sense to take the girl outta school halfway through, Bernie."

"Hush, Larry."

"You know you agree with me."

"Agreeing with you doesn't change it. It is not your choice or mine. Now hush, this is hard enough."

Larry threw his arms up in the air. "I'll be in the garage then."

Ondrea came down the stairs holding Vivi's hand. Sean followed them carrying a duffel bag.

"Do you have everything, Dear?" Nana B asked.

"I think so." Ondrea was doing her best to hold back her tears.

"Well, if you do leave something behind, you can always get it when you come and visit." Nana B zipped her coat up for her and they hugged.

Loretta came up next for a hug. "Take care of yourself, Ondrea."

"I will." Ondrea pulled away to pick Vivi up. "I'll miss you."

"I'll miss you more." Vivi held her tightly.

One tear escaped from Ondrea upon hearing her little voice. The sound of a car pulling up was then heard.

"I'll go put this in the car for you." Sean walked outside.

Ondrea followed to see Larry approaching from the garage.

He put his arms around her. "Ya know, I got used to having you around here."

"I got used to it, too."

Eirene opened the trunk of her gray Lexus to allow Sean to put the duffel bag away. "I wanted to say thank you to you all again for taking such good care of Ondrea. You have no idea what it means to me."

"She was a joy to have around," Loretta replied.

Ondrea walked over to Sean. "I didn't get to say goodbye to Rick. Can you tell him for me?"

"I will," Sean promised.

They hugged awkwardly before she got into the car. Eirene and Ondrea waved as they started to drive off. Sean didn't take his eyes off Ondrea. He regretted not telling her what he wanted to say last night because he had lost his nerve in the morning.

Suddenly, the car stopped, and Ondrea came flying out of it, running back to Sean. She stopped one foot away from him. "You were supposed to tell me something." She wiped tears from her eyes.

He breathed out one word, "Ethereal."

"What?" She looked confused.

"It's one of our bonus vocabulary words. It means too perfect for this world." He took a deep breath. "It's you."

Sean had just finished his last word when Ondrea leaned in and kissed him.

Larry and Bernadette chuckled at the sight, while Loretta's eyes grew double in size. Before Sean could catch his breath, she was back in the car driving away again. He felt more satisfied with that goodbye.

"Are you coming in or going for a run?" Loretta called to him.

"Going for a run."

Sean didn't feel like running, but he decided to keep his promise to Ondrea. He ran straight to Rick's house. He rang the bell and knocked a few times. He assumed Rick was home since his truck was in the driveway. Sean tried the doorknob, but it was locked. He peered through the window but didn't see anyone. But what he did see filled him with terror. Rick's coat was back. It was there hanging on a hook. Suddenly Sean could feel the world's rotation. Images of Rick and Marcus flooded his mind, then of Paladin and Bao.

When the answer finally hit Sean, he knew he couldn't waste another second.

Chapter 63

When Sean stepped into the house, Loretta saw the distress on her son's face at once. "What's wrong? Is it Ondrea?"

Sean tried to speak, but he realized that he didn't know what to tell her. The truth was not an option, not at that moment anyway. "I need to get to Marcus."

"I thought you decided not to do the fan club president thing."

"I need to get there. I left my homework folder there and I'll get a zero for the work!" Sean panicked.

"Okay, Honey. I'll drive you." She grabbed her coat.

Sean stepped outside to wait for her. The cold air felt like it was strangling his lungs.

She came out of the house, and they hustled to the jeep. "It needs to warm up a minute." She waited a second before she said, "I'm a little surprised you're this worried about your schoolwork."

"I ... I just wanna get good grades."

Vivi appeared outside the house wearing her snow boots and winter jacket.

"What is she doing?" Sean adjusted his seatbelt.

Larry could be seen waving as he held the screen door open.

Loretta waved back. "I guess she wants to come for the ride."

"No, mom. She can't," Sean ordered.

"Why not?"

He didn't know how to answer that question.

"Sean, you're acting very strange right now." Loretta got out to help Vivi into her booster seat.

Sean ground his teeth as he waited.

When they finally arrived, Marcus' house looked deserted. Everything that made it look like a home had been taken down. The curtains, windchimes, welcome mat, even the flag with the red sun were all gone. There was a U-Haul truck in the driveway.

"I didn't know he was moving?"

"Please stay in the car, Mom," Sean pleaded.

"Okay." Loretta shrugged somewhat annoyed.

Sean stepped out of the jeep and walked up to the house. The door was ajar, so he took it upon himself to enter. People were packing up in every room. There was only one person Sean recognized among the sea of workers. He went up to a man that he remembered from the store. Alec was delicately placing small figurines of Paladin into newspapers. "Excuse me. Do you remember me? From the store?"

Alec looked around, and at the sight of too many witnesses, shook his head.

Sean didn't have time to interrogate him, so he only asked, "Is Marcus here?"

Alec pointed to the kitchen. Sean followed that direction. He pushed the swinging door gently open to see Maeve sitting at the kitchen table staring out the window. She didn't seem to notice him, even when he stood right in front of her.

"Maeve?" Sean called out to her timidly.

She turned her head to look at him, then back to the window. "He's not here."

"Where is he?"

Maeve ignored his question.

"I know Rick is with him." She still didn't respond, so he said, "I know Paladin is with him."

Maeve gave him a sliver of her attention at the sound of the name. "Yes. He is."

"I need to know where to find them. Where are they?" More confident now, Sean moved closer to her.

Maeve once again disregarded the question.

"I know what he plans to do with him."

She laughed lightly then questioned him in a condescending tone, "What do you think you know?"

"If I wasn't a kid, I probably wouldn't believe this, but I know that Marcus is Bao."

Maeve tried not to react, but Sean saw her eyes constrict just enough to know she was rattled.

"I know he faked his death."

Maeve swallowed hard. "You sound ridiculous."

"I know he set Arjun up to get hurt that day on the ice."

Maeve glared at him. "You're right. Only a child would believe this nonsense."

"He was willing to sacrifice Arjun to find Paladin."

Maeve couldn't stop one tear from escaping and falling down her cheek as she continued to stare outside. Sean took another step closer to see what she was watching. It was Arjun playing in the snow with a woman by his side, guarding him.

She spoke softly, "He's safe now. Now that he has Paladin, no one else has to die." Maeve wiped the sudden stream of tears falling down her face and tightened her jaw. "It's over now. Arjun is safe."

"You'll never be safe with someone like that around."

Maeve peered into Sean's eyes.

He knew she was vulnerable, so he took his shot. "How many has he sacrificed to find Paladin?"

There was a long pause before she finally spoke again. "Growing up I wondered why my mother was always so cold. Never felt a hug, a goodnight kiss, never even a kind word. I thought that was just the way she was. All I had was my brother. Then he became old enough and I knew. I knew it because it was on her face. She never got close enough to feel for him or for anyone. She turned her heart to stone."

"He did this to your brother too?" Sean was trying to understand.

She breathed out hard. "I never wanted Arjun. After my brother's death, I swore that I would never have a child and feel that pain again. I tried hard to ignore Arjun's father, but David was so persistent."

"He killed Arjun's father?"

"No, it has to be family." In a sarcastic tone, she continued, "It's the great honor of the family. To sacrifice for him. For the greater power." She paused and placed her hand on the window where Arjun could be seen. "Truth is, he would be exposed otherwise. People would find out who he is and what he has done. David doesn't even know about Arjun. When I found out I was pregnant, I left him without a word, not even a note. I tried to disappear. But he found us."

"We can stop Bao."

"It's not Bao," she hissed. "I buried my father a long time ago."

Sean's head was spinning. "Wait. How long has this been going on?"

"Too long. It almost ended once with my father. My grandparents tried to save him. When he was seven years old, they gave him away to protect him."

The image of the foster home flashed in Sean's head. "How did Bao know about Paladin then?"

"He grew up outside of the family, but he remembered the stories from his youth."

Sean stared at her perplexed, unable to put the pieces together yet.

"The stories told by his great-grandfather. The stories Mortalan told."

The words hit Sean like a blow to the stomach. "Marcus is Mortalan?"

"The comics my father wrote are the reasons he's dead. That's how Mortalan was able to find him." Maeve saw the torment in Sean's eyes and decided to be merciful. "That's why he needed Paladin."

"He used his own family to stay young." Sean felt the spinning of the Earth once again and needed to grip the kitchen chair in front of him to stop from falling. He tried his hardest to control himself, but in the next second he was throwing up in the kitchen sink.

Maeve stood up to hand him a napkin.

Sean wiped his mouth. "Paladin isn't immortal. Mortalan will have to kill again eventually."

Maeve turned away from him. "Arjun is safe and that is all I care about."

Sean turned the faucet on and rinsed his mouth. "What about Arjun's children or grandchildren? You've stopped your fear, but what about his?"

The words penetrated the wall that Maeve had built.

"What about their lives? And if he gets Paladin's power there will be no one to stop him." Sean pushed.

She breathed heavily as she turned to him. Her eyes changed. They were human again. It was like a light went on inside her. Maeve walked to the backyard door. "Arjun, come inside." She turned back to Sean. "I'll take you where they are."

Arjun and the woman came inside the house. Maeve spoke in Japanese to the woman, hugged Arjan as she told him to be good and kissed him goodbye, then gestured for Sean to follow her.

"My mom is probably wondering what's taking so long," Sean said as she led the way.

"What are you going to tell her?" Maeve stepped outside the house with Sean beside her.

"I'm not really sure what..." Sean froze when he saw that their jeep was empty. "Where's my mother? Where's Vivi?" He looked around frantically.

Maeve did not move. She did not speak. She did not react in any way because she already knew.

Sean saw the expression on her face. He didn't have to ask, but he did anyway. "He has them?"

Only her eyes answered.

Chapter 64

Maeve drove recklessly, but it still wasn't fast enough for Sean. An hour later, they made it to their destination. Sean was not surprised by the look of it. There was an open field covered in snow next to the only building that could be seen for miles in any direction. Southeast of the building was a helicopter and on the other side was a row of vehicles. Sean spotted their jeep parked in front of the other cars. From the outside, the facility looked abandoned, except for the two-armed guards standing at the entrance. Sean was filled with fear at the sight of the weapons, but Maeve seemed unfazed. "Don't talk unless I tell you to," she told him.

"There has to be at least fifty floors." Sean's eyes followed the building's levels to the top.

"Remember don't talk. The only reason you're here is because I believe you are the only one who can get Paladin to change his mind. The Katorein is on the thirteenth floor," she spoke firmly. "That's where we need to get to."

Sean's eyes dilated. "The actual Katorein?"

"I thought I told you not to talk."

Sean went silent.

As they approached the building, Sean slowed his step to let her take the lead. She walked up to the guards as if she was supposed to be there, and Sean followed with his head down. She entered the facility, with greetings in Japanese towards the two men. They acknowledged her with a head nod and paid no mind to Sean.

The inside of the facility looked nothing like the outside. It was bright, clean, and looked new. The discrepancy reminded Sean of Irruption Comics. He followed Maeve to the elevator. As she pulled out a key from her pocket and inserted it, footsteps could be heard in the distance advancing towards them. Two different men stood in front of them now. The light to the elevator clicked on. One of the men spoke Japanese into the walkie-talkie. Maeve hit the button to go up. The man put the walkie-talkie away and spoke directly to Maeve. She responded. Sean couldn't understand a word. All he knew was that it was aggressive on both parts.

Two more guards came out from the other side of the corridor. One grabbed Sean by his right arm tightly. The other put his hand on Maeve gently. The security began escorting the intruders back from where they entered. The ding of the elevator could be heard in the background. All four men turned back to the distraction.

Maeve seized her chance. She side-kicked the guard holding her, knocking him off his feet. Then she chopped one in the throat, grabbed his gun while he gasped for air, and proceeded to hit the third man with that weapon. Before the guard holding Sean could react she was already pointing the gun at him. He had only managed to put his hand on his holster. She spoke firmly to the man. Sean knew her threat was serious. The guard must have known as well because he let go of Sean and put his gun on the floor. Maeve looked over at Sean. "Run!" She didn't have to say it twice.

Sean flew across the hallway and almost slipped trying to get into the elevator as the door was closing. He hit the thirteenth-floor button before he caught his breath.

*****

When the elevator door opened, Sean could hear Marcus speaking. They were in a room that showed silhouettes from the outside. Rick was easily identified by his build. Sean went into stealth mode as he slowly and cautiously proceeded. Unfortunately, his stealth mode still needed work. Before he was two feet from the room, a guard could be heard behind him clicking his tongue in a patronizing, disapproving manner. Then the man used his gun to do the rest of the talking for him.

When Sean entered the room with the guard behind him, it was only Rick who seemed surprised. Either Marcus had been told of their arrival or just assumed that Maeve would eventually betray him, because his face said, "I was expecting you." Behind Marcus were two women and one man in lab coats, working to prep what could only be the Katorein.

"Sean, what are you doing here?" Rick sounded angry but concerned. He sounded like a parent.

"I could ask you the same thing," he scowled as he spat. "I can't believe you would do this."

Ashamed, Rick responded, "I'm sorry kid, I'm just not cut out for this."

Strategically hiding his weapon, the guard forced Sean to sit in a chair in the corner.

"He's tricking you, Rick. He's not who you think he is."

"I assure you; this is Mr. Neige's decision. He came to me of his own accord," Marcus said as he signaled to one of the women to prep Rick.

"It's true, Sean." Rick allowed the woman to guide him to a medical bed. She began to place electrodes over his chest and arms.

At the sight, Sean's demeanor changed. "Rick, please don't do this. I'm sorry for what I said. I'm sorry for everything. Please just don't do this."

Marcus laid in the bed on the other side of the Katorein and allowed the male personnel to hook him up to the machine. Sean went to jump up, but the guard forced him to stay put. Upon witnessing this, Rick turned his attention to the guard. "Take your hands off of him."

"He can't understand you, Mr. Neige."

Rick stared at the guard; eyes locked in on him. "I think he can."

The guard took his hand off Sean's shoulder.

"Marcus, if I could just have a moment with Sean to explain things better."

"This child will never understand because he is just that, a child. It would be better to just have him removed from the area completely," Marcus insisted. He spoke in Japanese to the guard as he waved his hand in a dismissive tone.

Following orders, the guard lifted Sean to his feet. "Make sure you put me where you're keeping my mother and sister," Sean shouted.

"What?!" Rick looked back and forth between Sean and Marcus. "Loretta and Vivi are here? Why are they here?"

"Ask your new best friend. He's the one who brought them here." Sean struggled as the guard tried to remove him, triggering the man to press the gun into Sean's back.

"Marcus, what's going on? What is he talking about?"

Marcus only spoke in Japanese. Following commands, the attendants began working faster.

"Marcus, answer me!"

"He brought them here because he's the bad guy! Did you lose your common sense when you lost your memory?! Look around you! How many good guys you know need to be surrounded by men with guns?" Sean moved to the left to reveal the guard's weapon.

Rick sprang from the bed. He growled as he started tearing off the electrodes without breaking any eye contact with the man holding Sean. A loud humming noise could be heard as the Katorein was turned to maximum level.

Sean started shouting above the noise, "He's the bad guy! He's the villain!"

The attendants tried to stop Rick from pulling the EKG pads off completely.

Sean was screaming at the top of his lungs now, "He's Mortalan!"

At hearing his true name, Mortalan yelled something quick. Immediately one of the female attendants pulled a lever down and another lever up.

"Whose Mort..." Rick was unable to finish his sentence. His body was elevated off the ground. The Katorein was doing what it was created to do.

"I have not heard that name in so long. It's bittersweet." Marcus signaled to the guard, who then used the bottom of his gun to hit Sean on the back of his head. Sean fell to the floor. Before he lost consciousness, he could still see Rick attempting to get free.

"It's working. I can feel it!" Marcus called out as he slowly tilted his head back closing his eyes.

Rick tried desperately to do something, anything but was unable to move his body more than an inch in any direction. Sean was unsure how much time had passed when he opened his eyes again. A bright orange and white light was coming from Rick. It was blinding. The guard behind him was covering his eyes, so he did not notice as Sean pushed up on his knees to throw his elbow back in the most inconvenient area for any male.

In the next second, the guard was on his knees next to Sean, then on the ground holding his bruised region. Sean wasted no time. He ran, squinting, straight toward the Katorein. He tried to pull either of the levers back to their original place, but it was useless. He quickly gave up and ran back for his chair. Sean swung with all his might again and again. The attendants started to rush over to stop him, but his last swing had damaged something in the machine. The light began to come out of the Katorein as well as Rick. The attendants ran from the blinding light. Sean would have moved as well, but the Katorein had now claimed him.

Maybe Sean took some of the brunt of the pain or maybe the sight of Sean in agony made Rick stronger. Whatever the reason, Rick willed himself to the ground. Then he proceeded to pound on that contraption with all his strength. It was working because Marcus woke in a panic. The Katorein began to tremble uncontrollably.

"Stop him!" Marcus ordered in a weakened state.

The guard got to his feet and started charging, but Rick grabbed him by the throat. He held him in the air for a moment before flinging him across the room at the attendants. The humming from the Katorein had now turned into a shriek. Realizing the imminent danger, Rick staggering, picked Sean up and held him in his arms. The more distance Rick created between him and the unstable machine, the stronger he began to feel again.

Sean started to rouse. He looked at Rick and smiled. "Can we go home now, please?"

"Sounds good to me, kid."

"Paladin!"

Rick turned around to see Marcus crawling slowly on the floor clenching his teeth. But he wasn't Marcus anymore. Still attached to what was left of the Katorein, he shouted, "This isn't over!"

There was a ding as the elevator door opened next to them. Maeve stepped out. Upon seeing her, Rick held Sean in a defensive stance.

"It's okay. It's okay. She's on our side now."

Maeve gave a nod to Rick that he slowly returned.

"I found your mother and sister. They're outside waiting. I also found something else."

Rick stepped into the elevator with Sean. The floor under the Katorein began to give.

"Maeve!"

Maeve turned around to see Mortalan on his knees reaching out for her.

"Help me!" he cried.

She took a step backward into the elevator and let the door close on his screams.

Chapter 65

The three of them ran out of the facility as it started to cave in on itself. Loretta was standing outside, holding Vivi tightly in her arms while surrounded by guards. They were shaking, but one could not tell if it was from the cold or the fear. Rick hesitated as he gave a frustrated breath. Sean had Rick put him back on his feet.

"Don't worry. They work solely for me now." Maeve walked in front of them.

She spoke to the men, and they dispersed.

"How did you get..." Sean was in awe.

"I simply pointed out that I am the future, and he is the past."

"Works for me." Sean shrugged his shoulders.

Rick knew what was coming next, so he instructed everyone to back up to a safe distance. They watched the building collapse with Mortalan and the Katorein still inside. Sean had never before felt so much peace at the sight of so much destruction.

With a mixture of anger and panic in her voice, Loretta stammered, "Can you tell... Please, anyone... Can you tell me what the hell is going on here?"

"Mommy, you said a bad word."

"Hush, Vivi."

Sean looked to Rick for guidance, who unfortunately was looking at him for the same reason. Suddenly, a thunderous crack could be heard within the gravel behind them. In that moment, everyone knew they were not out of the woods yet.

Maeve rushed to her vehicle and opened the truck. She pulled out Verendus as Mortalan emerged from the wreckage. He ripped what was left of the electrodes off and padded some of the dust away. Maeve tossed Verendus to Rick, who caught it in his left hand as Mortalan approached.

"Sean, get your mother and sister to safety." Without hesitation, Rick went to protect what he loved.

"One last battle between old friends." Mortalan bowed slightly to Rick.

"It's over, Marcus."

"I have enough power to defeat you this time." Mortalan tore his shirt off with one hand. He was no longer a feeble old man but looked as young as Rick now. He tightened his muscles as he affirmed, "This will be our last fight."

"I'm going to make sure of that." Rick spun Verendus in his hand and swung at Mortalan, who caught it and lowered it down forcing Rick to lower his body as well. He kept his grip as he kneed Rick in the face. Then released as he pushed Rick in the chest with his right foot. The force sent Rick, Verendus, and debris across what was left of the building.

Rick jumped back onto his feet. He grunted and charged full speed toward Mortalan, who was also sprinting, ready to play chicken. Rick wound his left arm at the same time Mortalan wound his right. When their fists met in the middle, a concussive force pushed both of them backward, sliding on their feet in the snow.

In the distance, Sean and Maeve were seen ushering Loretta and Vivi into Maeve's car. Before Rick could stop him, Mortalan seized the opportunity, picking up a railing that was close by and sending it sailing through the air. Maeve had started driving, but they only made it a few feet when the railing crashed into the ground right before them, which would have prevented even the most skilled driver from avoiding the collision. Rick became distracted as he witnessed the wreck and watched to ensure that everyone exited the vehicle unharmed.

Mortalan once again saw the opportunity that presented itself. He picked up an enormous piece of pavement and threw it like it was a Frisbee. Rick had barely any time to react. He caught it, but it forced him to his knees. In the next second, Mortalan slammed his entire body on top of the massive boulder, forcing Rick on his back, stealing his breath from his lungs.

"You really aren't him anymore." Mortalan laughed as he slowly leaned in. "When I'm finished with Maeve, I'm going to break the boy," he purred.

At these words, Rick conjured all of his power from his old life. Slowly he picked up the great piece of foundation while getting back on his feet, causing Mortalan to lose his balance and fall back to the earth. A shadow was cast upon him from Rick holding the monstrous block above his own head. For a moment, the sight left Mortalan awestruck. In an epic show of strength, Rick brought the colossal rock down, crashing it into his left knee, and breaking it in half. A fire of anger burned in Rick's eyes and Mortalan could now feel that heat.

"I've come too far to give up now." It was unclear if Mortalan was speaking to Rick or himself. He jumped up and swung his right fist, but the hero caught it. He tried with his left but that move was futile as well. Rick slowly but effortlessly brought both of Mortalan's hands down. In the next moment, Mortalan felt the complete impact of the great warrior's head against his own.

Temporarily unconscious, Mortalan was unaware that Rick had picked him up over his head until he was already diving back to the ground. Sean remembered the same move in issue seven, *Paladin: The End of an Era*. It was when Paladin fought Hirendan for the last time. He wondered if Rick remembered. If somehow some part of him still remembered who he was.

Rick stood over the lifeless body of Mortalan. In the distance, he could hear Vivi cheering for him. Mortalan's body was draped over an edge of a wall. Rick breathed in and out as he waited for any sign of life, when none was given he began walking away from a piece of his past towards the complete picture of his future.

Playing possum, Mortalan slid his right hand down to the side of his calf. He yanked his pant leg up, revealing a strapped knife that was the length from his knee to his ankle. Maeve could be seen in the distance, shaking her head at Rick's grave mistake. Her gesture made Rick realize his fallacy. Mortalan was ready for round two.

In his peripheral vision, Rick could see the obsidian steel calling to him. He tightly grasped the tool that was made for him, for he was still determined to defend what was his. Once again, they met halfway, battling in rapid strikes and blocks. Mortalan was relentless. Swinging, again and again, to draw blood from the champion. His success was only shown in a single swipe that left crimson shimmering across Rick's chest.

"So, Paladin does bleed."

Rick took a deep breath, spun Verendus, and struck Mortalan in his right arm as he was preparing to make another wound on the other than flawless skin. The knife made a loud, clicking sound as it fell to the ground. At once, Mortalan leaped to obtain his weapon, but only received Rick's knee to his face. He was falling back, but Rick grabbed him by his hair to steady him and then swung Verendus backhanded across the left side of Mortalan's face. The blow made him lose his footing, but not for long.

Mortalan was now standing again but had lost some of his newfound bravado. Rick spun Verendus around his left hand, ready for the last round. Mortalan, not wanting to be defenseless, picked up a nearby two-by-four. Rick instantly chopped the wood in half, before Mortalan could make a fighting stance. Gripping Verendus with both hands, Rick struck Mortalan in the jaw with the bo in a downward motion, then reversed his direction striking him again as he came back up, causing blood to spray from his mouth.

Mortalan tried to create distance between him and the great force in front of him, but Rick used Verendus to take his feet out from under him. His face now in the dirty snow, Mortalan did what any villain would do. Without an ounce of honor, he closed his hand on some of the sediments in the snow that laid before him and flung them into the hero's face. Blinded,

Rick dropped Verendus. Seizing the moment, Mortalan lunged for the prized possession. He picked it up and immediately swung it, smashing the instrument into the back of Rick's hard skull. The hit sent him flying face first into half of a wall that was still standing. Rick took out a quarter of the concrete as he flew through it like it was made of Styrofoam.

Sean and the others could do nothing but stand there as an audience. Maeve had over a dozen men standing at her command, but she knew they were useless in this battle between the titans. No, this fight beckoned to be just between the two.

"Oh, the covenanted weapon of the great Paladin. I searched the seven continents for more than half a century for this beautifully forged work of art." Mortalan showed off his skills with the bo.

Rick was up, holding what was left of the wall to balance.

"The old Paladin would never have let me get close enough to lay even a finger on it. I guess he's gone forever."

At that moment, Verendus began lighting up. The matte black bo was now glowing red. Intrigued, Mortalan froze to watch the magnificent display of color change. In the next second, he was screaming as spikes came out in exactly the same placement where his hands laid upon the Damascus steel. Mortalan dropped Verendus, and the spikes immediately retracted. Not wasting his chance, Rick ran and picked it up. Mortalan stood up, prepared to fight with his hands dripping with blood. Rick once again swiped his feet. Mortalan almost hit the ground, but Rick punched him as he was in mid-air, slamming him into the rest of the wall that was left standing. Before Mortalan could react, Rick was in front of him pressing Verendus against his throat, increasing the pressure slowly. Rick stood there watching Mortalan grow weaker and weaker. He saw the life leaving his dark eyes.

"He's not stopping," Loretta whispered.

At these words, Sean sprinted to get to Rick. Loretta tried to catch him, but Sean was gone within that second.

"Wow, Sean's so fast," Vivi said with her eyes wide. Loretta turned to Maeve, who was also thunderstruck by the sight of his speed. Sean was now standing next to Rick and Mortalan.

"Rick, you have to stop." Sean pleaded.

"He won't stop. He won't ever stop. You heard him." Rick didn't blink or turn his head.

"You have to stop." Sean put his hands gently on Rick's left arm.

"Why? Why should I?"

"Because you're not like him. Because you're the good guy."

"I'm not Paladin." Rick shook his head.

"I know." Sean paused. "You're Rick."

Rick turned his head to make eye contact with Sean. He grinded his teeth and grunted, but finally released Mortalan. He hit him once more with the end of Verendus for good measure. Sirens could now be heard in the far distance.

"Come on. The police are coming. They'll handle him." Sean gestured with his head for them to leave.

Neither one of them had noticed Maeve coming up on the side. She stood over the limp body of Mortalan with only one thought inside her head. Sean and Rick were walking away when they heard the two gunshots. They turned to see Maeve holding one of the guard's guns in her hand.

She turned to face them. "You were right. He was never going to stop."

Police vehicles were now visible in the distance. Rick placed Verendus down leaning against a column by them.

"You should go." She threw the gun down and walked over to them. "I'll handle the mess here."

Rick looked over at Loretta who was still shielding Vivi from the sound of the gunshots.

"Once people find out who you are, or who you were… they will never leave you alone. It's better to lay low for a while until this blows over."

Rick looked at Sean, who was staring at the ground.

"Go while you still have a chance," Maeve urged.

Sean looked up and saw the police cars approaching. He knew Rick's window to escape was becoming smaller and smaller.

He finally turned to him. "She's right. You should go."

"How? The cars are demolished, and I can't fly, remember."

"Take the helicopter." Maeve called two guards over and told them to take Rick to a safe location. She made sure she spoke in English to ensure the transparency of her intentions. One guard ran to the helicopter and started it up.

By this time Loretta, still holding Vivi, had walked over. "Is someone going to explain all of this to me?" Loretta's voice broke.

"I will, Mom. I promise, just not right now."

Loretta looked over at the helicopter and then at Rick, who hadn't taken his eyes off her since she appeared. "You're leaving, aren't you?" she asked softly.

Rick went to speak, but Sean interrupted. "He has to, Mom. For now."

A tear started to fall from Loretta's eye, but before it made its way down her cheek, Rick caught it.

"This is why you were acting so strange, huh?"

Rick's eyes answered for him.

"You're leaving?" Vivi's lip quivered.

Rick kissed Vivi on the head. "Yes, but not for long."

Seeing the police almost upon them, Maeve announced, "It's now or never."

Rick leaned over to Loretta's ear and whispered something that was inaudible to the others. The words brought more tears to her eyes. Then he kissed her on the cheek as she bit her lip to stop from crying.

"Goodbye, Sean."

"Goodbye, Rick."

Rick began walking off with the guard following behind him. Sean's thoughts were racing. Suddenly, he shouted, "Wait!"

Rick stopped before entering the helicopter, his hair waving wildly in the wind. Sean ran faster than ever before. He stood in front of Verendus, contemplating. Trusting his gut, he picked it up and flew over to Rick.

"Don't forget this," Sean said above the loud noise of the propellers.

Rick took Verendus from Sean, staring at him in awe. "How did you do that?"

Squinting his eyes from the wind he replied, "I was scared to lift Verendus, but I had to take the chance. Maybe it only hurts the bad guys, ya know."

"No, I mean how did you run so fast?" Rick signaled for Sean to turn around and see the puddles of water with steam still rising from where his feet had touched the snow. He looked down at his sneakers to see they were worn down to almost nothing. The sight made Sean just as amazed as the others, but before he could respond the guard told Rick they needed to go.

"Next time then." Rick smiled.

Sean nodded. Rick went to turn to climb into the helicopter, but Sean had thrown his arms around him. Rick placed his free hand on Sean's head. They held the embrace for a small moment. Sean pulled away and backed up to watch the helicopter take off. The police arrived just as Rick became indistinguishable in the air.

Epilogue

Dear Rick,

Maeve told me to write to you because she can't or won't tell us where you are. A lot has changed over the last month. Ondrea came back! Her Aunt owned some property out here and decided to make it their permanent home to make her happy. It's great having her around again, even if she doesn't live with me anymore. She even got the highest score on the English test the first day she was back in school. Mrs. Parker gave her the choice not to take it, but you know Ondrea. She was pretty upset when I told her everything that she missed. She said she would have been, in her words, of great assistance.

I joined the track team at school. Don't worry, though. I never go as fast as I can. Ondrea has a theory about that whole thing, but I'll let her tell you when you come back. Vivi is doing good. She keeps asking for you. She wants me to tell you that she found a new cat. He's an orange tabby that she named Gingee. Kind of a girl's name, but he seems to like it. Mom was sick for a while. She went to the doctor's office, but she won't tell us what he told her, except that it's good news. She said we have to wait until you come home to hear it. Nana B keeps smiling and telling mom to take it easy. To tell you the truth, I think Nana B figured it out. She always does. Or maybe she's just happy that Larry is better or something like that. Maeve says that you can't come back until she's finished handling the investigation. We all had to make statements, but I knew not to mention you-know-what, or you-know-who, or anything else. Vivi told them everything, but they just laughed and said she had quite the imagination. I hope you will come back soon. Everybody here misses you.

Be Safe,

Sean

P.S. I keep thinking. What or who else is real? You know what I mean.

www.ingramcontent.com/pod-product-compliance
Lightning Source LLC
Chambersburg PA
CBHW021409310726
48971CB00005B/1264